LONG JOHN
The Longest Stride

An inspirational biographical novel based on the Life and Times of
1936 "Hitler Olympics" Gold Medal Winner John Woodruff

DAVID ORANGE

D1547765

MILFORD
HOUSE
an imprint of Sunbury Press, Inc.
Mechanicsburg, PA USA

MILFORD HOUSE

an imprint of Sunbury Press, Inc.
Mechanicsburg, PA USA

NOTE: This is a work of fiction. Names, characters, places and incidents are the product of the author's imagination or are used fictitiously, and any resemblance to actual persons, living or dead, business establishments, events or locales is entirely coincidental.

For information about special discounts for bulk purchases, please contact Sunbury Press Orders Dept. at (855) 338-8359 or orders@sunburypress.com.

To request one of our authors for speaking engagements or book signings, please contact Sunbury Press Publicity Dept. at publicity@sunburypress.com.

FIRST MILFORD HOUSE PRESS EDITION: September 2020

Set in Adobe Garamond | Interior design by Crystal Devine | Cover design by Lawrence Knorr | Edited by Abigail Henson.

Publisher's Cataloging-in-Publication Data
Names: Orange, David, author.
Title: Long john : the longest stride / David Orange.
Description: First trade paperback edition. | Mechanicsburg, PA : Milford House Press, 2020.
Summary: The story of Olympic athlete John Woodruff who broke through racial barriers in the 1930s when he accompanied Jesse Owens to Berlin.
Identifiers: ISBN : 1-978-620063-87-3 (softcover).
Subjects: FICTION / African American / Historical | FICTION / Sports.

Product of the United States of America
0 1 1 2 3 5 8 13 21 34 55

Continue the Enlightenment!

Dedication

I would like to profoundly thank attorney at law, Mark Sorice, of western Pennsylvania. He and cousin filmmaker/actor Phil Coccioletti of Sugarcamp Productions Inc., New York City, were born and raised in Greensburg, Pennsylvania—only a few miles from John Woodruff country—Connellsville. Their lengthy filmed and oral interview with John Woodruff, several years ago, was designed by the three of them to use for a documentary film/biographical novel on the great runner and hero which Sorice hopes to be associate producer on its making. *Long John* used for its primary source John Woodruff's own words about his life, both on the track and off.

CHAPTER 1

Connellsville, Pennsylvania, 2001

John Woodruff was a kindly-faced, eighty-six-year-old black man, gracious, and with an articulate voice. He sat in a vehicle passenger's seat beside his equally kind eighty-year-old wife, Rose.

"How do you feel?" she asked.

Old John considered. "Excited to be going back home, visiting friends, and seeing you-know-who again."

Rose patted his hand.

Old John and his wife were driven into a small relic mining and steel industrial town. Inside the car, John took an extra-long look out the window to view the railroad yards along the Youghiogheny River or "the Yough" as the locals called it.

"Bring back memories?" Rose asked.

John smiled, seeing the image of a young black youth running on a cinder path alongside the locomotive engine chugging out of the station.

Arriving at Falcon Football Stadium in Connellsville, Old John guided his wheelchair to the south end of the stadium, where he gazed nostalgically at a majestic near 80-foot high oak tree that had stood since 1936, its elongated branches creating a sheltering canopy.

"I'd like a little time with my tree, hon. Come by in a bit, okay?"

"I won't be far," she answered, patting her husband on the shoulder before walking away.

The Woodruff Tree, Connellsville, PA

He situated his chair and his small portable tank with a nasal cannulas by his side just in case for oxygen before gazing at a broad sign reading:

JOHN WOODRUFF 5K RACE/WALK – July 11 - 7 pm

Today they were celebrating the 19th anniversary of this race, created by John's boyhood South Connellsville friend and classmate, Peter Salatino. In 1982, he and some of his friends convinced townsfolk, also proud of Woodruff's accomplishments, that they needed something to stand as a testament to their local hero's Berlin Olympics greatness.

Years ago, John started a scholarship fund for the high school kids of the Connellsville area. He was able to raise six thousand dollars to get it started, and it has been in existence for nearly twenty years. Every year the foundation would give a one thousand-dollar check to the outstanding male and female in the high school as well as benefiting charities in the area.

In the sixty-eight years since the Woodruff tree was planted, not only had it presided over thousands of scholastic events at the stadium, it was recognized each year at the start of a race in his honor: the John Woodruff 5K (3 miles) Run/Walk. It began on Arch Street and ended at Connellsville Stadium.

To John and many others, the event stimulated a lot of the kids, igniting them to do well. And for John to be a part of a youth's interest in track was one of the greatest treasures of his long life. It was as if he had come to understand that listening to teens and helping them with their problems—on-field and off—was one of the most important things he could do in life. To him, if you cared, you listened. And he listened.

John eventually parked his chair near a plaque along the tree that read:

OLYMPIC OAK

WON BY

JOHN Y. WOODRUFF C.H.S. '35

BERLIN – 1936

PLAQUE BY THE DAILY COURIER

Old John's long fingers traced the plaque as he said to himself, "I'm thankful, Lord, that you've allowed me to return one last time."

Old John studied the track. Gone was the dusty cinder track of yore, replaced by a clean and bouncy synthetic one.

The aged man was snapped out of his reverie by a group of excited teens in athletic track attire between the ages of twelve to sixteen rushing toward him.

Their phones clicked away, taking selfies and videos with the living legend.

A boy proudly exclaimed, "Mr. Woodruff, later on, I'm gonna show you what I've got. Keep your eye on me, sir!"

That had Old John chuckling, "Oh, I think I can see what you have already."

The runners made some smart moves to imaginary music.

John with young runners at John Woodruff 5K race/walk

An Asian girl of twelve, as cute as a button with dimples and an animated voice, crisp but still a bit on the shy side approached John. She eased into asking, "Can I ask a question? My mom always says not to be rude, but . . . your legs must've been the most important thing in your life."

John answered kindly, "Yes, they were."

"How does it feel," she hedged, "you know . . . hard for you even to walk."

"Well, I'm here," Old Woodruff said without hesitation. "My legs are just a part of me. You don't lose your essence of who you are because a part is not working so well, right?"

"I guess not," the Asian girl said apologetically. "I still think it's a real tragedy."

Woodruff then changed the subject by taking a photo from a manila envelope.

It was a caricature sketch by a newspaper writer and artist that exaggerated Young John's unnaturally long, running stride to the point of actually elongating his rubber-like legs to seemingly "twice" their length.

The group found the sketch amusing.

EDWARDS (Canada)   Woodruff (U.S.A)

Long John Woodruff caricature of his elastic-like long stride winning the Berlin Olympics.

With his blue-gray eyes still full of life, Old John began retelling stories that never got old.

"Sportswriters had a field day with my long stride," he informed. "Now, I'm giving these old photos to the Woodruff Track Club."

"Was it really nine feet, sir?" another teen asked. "That's gotta be exaggerated."

"That was my stride, maybe even a tad more at times. I was all leg."

The excited teens tried to calculate on the grass the distance of John's stride. They took turns running and falling over each other laughing, but no one came remotely close to matching it.

The Asian girl gestured to the big tree shading them. "They say you brought this tree here when it was a baby."

"Yep, all the way from the Berlin Olympics. A gift to Gold Medal winners from Adolf Hitler. It carries significance for many people who come from all over to visit it."

"Are you the oldest living Gold Medalist from those Olympics?"

"That I am," John answered. "All the others have died. Many became terrific friends of mine."

Another teen spoke up. "I wanna hear about your famous race."

"Later, I promise. After the race."

A get together after the race today would, as usual, be held a Bud Murphy's Sports Bar. Glass souvenirs would be provided to race participants and filled-free for a couple of hours.

As in previous years, when John attended this 5K event, cameras would be clicking everywhere, and many runners and fans would pose with John as he signed autographs before sounding off the starting gun and later crowning the victors. And to the first seven-hundred and fifty finishers, they would receive replicas of Woodruff's Berlin Gold Medal.

These youngsters would participate in the race/walk event in the early evening but were already in their track attire. Knowing all about John's stellar track reputation, these kids were no different from all others across the country that John had spoken to over the years. Sometimes, as now, with their enthusiasm running high, Woodruff took on cult status. To them, this man became revered in the lofty atmosphere of mythical Paul Bunyan or Superman. But above all that, they knew Woodruff's story and values were from a bygone American era when heroes were not always out of comic books, or the ones who made the most money in big movies and whatnot. They were people who did things such as personal sacrifice gain for the betterment of all, or ones who gave their word and stuck to it.

John told the group, "Right now, can I see you all hit the track and run like the wind? I'll see you all later."

The kids rushed over to the track, except for the teen girl who stayed by Woodruff.

"You don't want to run?" he asked.

"I'd rather sit here because I have to leave with my parents right after the race. Can I? Just for a bit . . . ?"

"I guess so if you don't mind sitting by an old man with broken down legs."

The girl lit up. "Not at all! Can you tell me some things about yourself, Mister Woodruff? Like when you were my age?"

JOHN WOODRUFF
NCAA CHAMPION — 880
1937-38-39
1936 U.S. OLYMPIC TEAM CHAMPION

John, mostly a private fellow all his life, was not that way with children who sought guidance from him. How could he not open up with these kids who had the passion for running as he once had? He hoped today that before they parted, this hopeful teen and others he would talk to later would separate John Woodruff, the man from the legend, from the myth.

"Were you a slave?" the teen girl asked.

Old John again chuckled before telling stories that never got old. "No, I wasn't. I once figured out that over the last seventy years, I told my story on average two times a day. That's fifty thousand times."

John looked about the stadium football field and beyond to some of the town's buildings. "I've run into some old friends who say the working conditions in Connellsville still aren't good," John said. "But the town itself hasn't changed much. It's still beautiful to me, as are its people. I feel like my old gang was here only yesterday."

Old John found a bookmarker in his mind.

"You know, for every victory I had in my life," Old John continued, "there also came defeats. I guess everything happens for a reason, even the most disheartening setbacks. You see, you learn from them."

"Defeats like what?"

"They weren't in the running; that was the easy part," John answered. "I won ninety-eight percent of them. But once I left Connellsville for the great unknown, the color of my skin had me destined to meet Jim Crow."

"Jim Crow?" asked the listener. "What race did he run?"

"The segregation race," John answered. "After leaving Connellsville, where they treated me as an equal among my white friends, I was about to fraternize with my fellow black people. Together we met prejudice, something that had all blacks as second-class citizens."

Old John caught himself. "But first, let me start at the beginning. My parents were born free children of tobacco field slaves in Virginia," John said. "After the Civil War, my family ended up in South Connellsville, where I was born, the eleventh of twelve kids."

CHAPTER 2

Connellsville, Pennsylvania, 1923

Twelve-year-old Johnny was running about Connellsville as if a motor was attached to him. Head held back high, he flew through downtown, along the river, into the hills with trails, to school, and everywhere in between.

He whizzed by a senior couple in their eighties sitting on their porch, holding fly swatters.

"He goes past 'ere ever' day on the way to school, the senior man said. "Going home, ever' which way."

His wife agreed. "Never walkin', always runnin'."

"Yep," her senior husband agreed as he honed in on a fly to swat. "Gotcha!"

Young Johnny off in the distance abruptly stopped, sat on the ground, and took off a sneaker. A pebble had gotten through a hole in its sole.

The lad took out a small piece of flat rubber, sticking it into his shoe to plug the hole. Satisfied with his cleverness, Johnny bounced up and resumed his run.

CHAPTER 3

Landsberg, German State of Bavaria, 1923

At the same time as Young Woodruff was running, an intense, thirty-something Adolf Hitler, eyes piercing, did a slow two-finger dance on a manual typewriter. Alongside him was a stack of typed pages. He usually had a typist he would dictate to, but there were days when he was so fueled with energy that he often could not wait for help to arrive and did it himself. And today, he had a different kind of guest arriving.

The title page read: *Mein Kamph (My Struggle)*

Pleased with his prose, Hitler continued.

A short time later, he stopped to concentrate on another passage. He rose from his chair and stood as if giving a speech to an imaginary multitude.

"I am appalled at society, allowing blacks to become lawyers, teachers, even pastors," he spat. "It's criminal lunacy to keep on drilling a born half-ape while members of the highest culture-race must remain in unworthy positions."

Interrupting, a young animated voice dramatist coach, occultist, and supposed clairvoyant, and whatnot.

"*Herr* Hitler," Hanussen began, "you must learn to speak and move with authority. It's no different from an Olympic athlete practicing daily, so you must stretch your oratory muscles." Hanussen demonstrated by gesticulating with hand and arm movements as Hitler worked to mimic his style in front of a full-length mirror.

"That's better," Hanussen said in approval. "Open the hands more, then close into fists . . . let your power come through it, turn your eyes into magnets that seek out iron in the blood of people, control them."

Young Hitler's eyes glowed, his vortex energy whipping into a whirlwind delivery that became compelling.

Hanussen suggested, "Now give me an impromptu speech from something in your writings. Treat the audience as a sexual partner. Start

Hitler honing his oratory skills for acting coach in front of a mirror.

slow and soft, eventually picking up the pace and volume until the audience has reached its climax and all go home spent!"

Hitler, the mirror his audience, worked to summon a rousing speech, awakening an oratory force from somewhere deep inside of him.

Hanussen clapped in approval. "Outstanding, *Herr* Hitler. You've got the beginnings of a great public speaking instrument. Continue to perfect voice inflections and tone, and you'll have people eating out of your hand. Also, I suggest you study acting and perhaps hypnotism."

"Why?" Hitler asked.

"You'll soon be a performer in front of the largest stage imaginable. You must become a force never before seen, able to convince the German masses to ride a wave of nationalism, you the grandmaster who'll sweep Germans off their feet!"

Hitler caught up in zeal, eagerly went back to rehearsing.

CHAPTER 4

Connellsville, Pennsylvania, 2001

Through all the activities going on, Old John's soft-spoken voice honed by education retold his story.

"Times were hard in those days. We had a small farm, maybe three acres. My parents were just ordinary black people. They were not well educated and nearly illiterate but came here to do better. They weren't interested in my school. I used to sign my report card. But that's how things were at that time, especially for a black boy. I expected to end up in the mills."

The teen girl, alone, asked, "Were people mean to you because you were black?"

"Oh no," Old John answered with emphasis. "We all got along. There were only two black families in town and only four black students at the high school. So, I had nearly all-white playmates. They treated me no differently than anyone else."

Senior John told how he played with all white children, even ate meals at white family homes, and went to the movies with Caucasian kids.

He recalled, "Back then, we paid only five cents to get in downtown Connellsville's Big Top Movie Theater."

There were eight girls and four boys in the family of Silas and Sarah Woodruff. All the girls had lived to maturity, among them Mary Jones, who would live her life in South Connellsville. Two of John's older brothers, Clarence and Roger, had died in infancy, which was not un-common in those days. Several of his brothers had died young, including one killed while hunting.

"The farm was on the outskirts of Connellsville," John continued. "In the Gibson area called Reidmore. Back then, we called the area White Rock. We raised some hogs and chickens, and my mom planted vegetables for the family. I used to cut firewood and gather coal.

"Where I lived was mostly an all-white neighborhood," John continued. "And we got along fine. I was treated no differently than how anyone else was. Oh sure, we had our fights now and then, but I'd spend time at their homes such as I did with my good friend Pete Salatino. I ate a lot of spaghetti over there with his family, my favorite dish."

"Is that the man who started the John Woodruff 5K walk/run?"

"Yes, he was one of the team. And you know what?" John beamed. "Some acorns from this tree were planted in Pete and his wife's yard right here in Connellsville. One of them took, and an oak tree is now about twenty feet tall."

John recalled how the conditions at that time were the same for everybody. His mother, Sarah, took in washing from the white people around town, while also doing day work.

"What kinds of jobs did your father have when he came here?" the curious teen asked John.

"My dad Silas was a laborer. He dug coal and worked the steel mills and coke ovens in Connellsville, like the H.C. Frick Company. He also worked in nearby Clairton. That town was now depressed since the mills had closed decades ago."

Connellsville was at the center of the bituminous coal and coke in-dustries of southwestern Pennsylvania, with particular attention to the Connellsville Coke Region. Tucked along the base of the Chestnut Ridge in the Allegheny Mountains of southwestern Pennsylvania, the Con-nellsville Coke Region was world-famous for its abundant, high-quality bituminous coal and beehive coke. Geographically speaking, this area situated in a long narrow strip of land averaging three and a half miles wide and nearly forty miles long, stretching from Latrobe in Westmoreland County to the area around Smithfield in Fayette County.

During the coke and coal days, Connellsville had at one time more millionaires per capita than any other place in the country and possibly the world; this was when Connellsville was king of coal and coke with beehive ovens lighting up the hillsides. Railroads crisscrossed the city and streetcars connected neighborhoods and other towns. When Connellsville became a city in 1909, estimates had the population at more than 22,000.

The first successful oven ever built was only 300 feet from the old stone house erected by Zachariah Connell. That was the humble beginning of what grew into an industrial giant. The coke region ultimately would stretch 21 miles in either direction—north and south. In 1905, the area produced an amount of coke, which, if loaded on railroad freight cars, will make a train so long the engine in front will go from Connellsville to San Francisco and back before the caboose moves from the starting point!

"Dad also worked in a stone quarry. He was considered a powerful man, about 5'11", with considerable girth. I heard stories about him lifting stone slabs and rocks that generally required two or three men to do so."

John told of Connellsville once having several stone quarries that produced jobs for the people of the community in its early years. The first one opened in 1870 in the South Connellsville area. Another large one was the *Casparis Caverns,* located in the mountains above town.

"The mills and stone quarries were hard work, but my father didn't complain," John recalled. "Like everyone else with a family, Dad was just glad to have jobs to put food on the table."

"Did he also run track?"

"No," John informed. "But he could have or even been a weight-throwing man. Back in those days, there wasn't time to play sporting games. You had to spend all day working so you could have a roof over your head and food on the table. People worked much more than today's forty-hour workweek—thirteen days out of fourteen in the mills! Wages were meager, and families had more children than they do today."

"If your dad wasn't nearly as tall as you," the teen assessed, "where did you get your height?"

"I was built more like my mom, Sarah," Woodruff answered fondly. "She was tall, about five-foot-nine, and slim."

John also never forgot the words of an old *Connellsville Daily Courier* news editor, John Whoric, who said of John "Youie" Woodruff:

"I remember my first contact with Johnny Woodruff. Shortly after I was married, my wife became ill, and we needed a helping hand. Someone directed me to John's mother, and she agreed to do our family laundry. I remember vividly Johnny coming to our home on Sycamore Street, with a little wagon that he pulled to pick up the laundry, and then he drew that same wagon back after the washing and ironing. Johnny didn't only do that for us. His mother had quite a few customers, and Johnny never once complained that he was asked to help the family share its responsibilities."

Old John continued. "I think back to that time of my mom working all day long for two-and-a-half dollars. That's how things were back then.

"So, I didn't become associated with people of my color until after I graduated from high school," John continued. "Well, of course, I ran into a number of them after that. You see, I went to two different high schools. I went to one where it was just my immediate family. My niece and I attended this particular high school, and then I went my junior year to the city of Connellsville. That's where I got involved in athletics, you see."

"I know you graduated from Connellsville High," the girl said. "What was the name of the other school you went to?"

"Gibson High School," John answered. "All right, so to continue my high school education, I did freshman and sophomore years at the first high school, then to Connellsville High School in the city to start my junior year."

John added that school also became taught in three rented rooms in the "Brick Store." The building had been located at the corner of Park and Pittsburgh Street but was eventually torn down. He also told of the South Connellsville stockyards closing about 1967 when the livestock was prepared for market in the Midwest. The meat had begun being shipped by refrigeration cars.

John added, "That area also had some of the trails that my long stride had blazed from running."

"They run alongside the railroad tracks," the young listener knew. "I once read that you used to run to school and back home, never to walk. An' that you raced trains. That true?"

Old John closed his eyes, found a bookmarker in his mind, and recounted a tale of his youth.

CHAPTER 5

Connellsville, 1923

The spindly legs of the ebony-skinned eleven-year-old boy with patches about his jeans churned in long strides, his breathing deep but even. His feet landed onto the ground in precise thuds as he glided over the banks of the Youghiogheny River in the small coal mining community of Connellsville, in mountainous southwestern Pennsylvania fifty miles southeast of Pittsburgh. No one would ever imagine that this unknown boy, John Woodruff, would be nicknamed "Long John"; and have an essential date in history with a nemesis across the Atlantic who was just gaining notoriety for his ruthlessness and greed.

As young Johnny's legs churned, head held back, he breathed mostly through his nose instead of mouth—a sign of a conditioned runner much older than he. Running was in his blood, the beautiful, free feeling coming so naturally to him. For poor people like John, running was a sport where money did not matter. And John's family was poor indeed.

His feet meandered throughout the hillside area sprinkled with bee-hive-shaped coke ovens that were wide at the bottom and narrower at the top. He had learned early, mostly through helping bring in the ore to fire up the furnace at home, that the entire Fayette County was dependent on these precious ores for not only heating but employment.

Suddenly John stopped dead in his tracks, lifting afoot to better inspect his sneaker's sole that had sprung another hole, this one large enough for a stone to dig through the rubber and into his skin. He sat on the ground to take off the shoe, took from his back pocket a piece of cardboard, folded it, and slid it into the sneaker to plug up the gap, and resumed running.

After traversing through winding, hilly dirt roads, the boy veered back down towards the town's railroad stockyard. The massive facility built by the Baltimore and Ohio Company on the outskirts of town gave employment to many men in the South Connellsville area since it became a stopover to feed, water, and rest the animals shipped from the Midwest for food back East.

Young John was used to the smell of the one-hundred open pens for cattle, sheep, and hogs since over two thousand cars of livestock were fed and watered per month at these stockyards.

Along one stretch of the yard away from the slower freight cars, a locomotive spun on rails crisscrossing the city. Young John reined in his skittish nerves and ran on a narrow cinder path parallel to the train. He heard the locomotive churning, hissing, and steaming from behind, bearing down on him.

The engineer—a burly, unshaven white man with a red scarf around his neck and chewing a big wad of tobacco wore a blunt expression. His pulling on a rope sounded a shrill whistle, warning the boy to get out of the way.

The menacing machine and its driver intimidated John, but he forced himself not to back off from the tracks, finally finding the courage to take it on in a race.

As the locomotive built up steam, its tremendous force thundering toward him, the boy pushed down the butterflies in his stomach. John's skinny legs moved piston-like, but they did not have the firepower to keep up with the train's gathering force. Once the mass of metal caught up to him, its conductor again blew the whistle. To the youth, the shrill blaring toot meant to say, *Nice try, kid, but you lost!*

The train roared out of the yard, kicking up pebbles and cinders into the lad's face.

John accepted defeat but also learned something from this loss. Just facing that monster was sort of a victory in itself. It made him realize there was nothing to fear but fear itself. He would race this train differently the next time. The boy could assess his running abilities accurately. In all the races with his gang of white youths, he was the fastest and won against them handily. But how fast was he? Indeed, racing a train was biting off more than he could chew. Someday when he would grow in size, his stride would lengthen, and he visualized beating that monstrous, menacing locomotive.

As John continued running towards town, his mind stored away from the blueprints of the race. The next time they battled, he knew to be more relaxed, keep an inner focus, maintain form, and will himself to find a rhythm.

He entered South Connellsville. The year was 1923, and streetcars, autos, and horse-drawn buckboards moved about their business. Pittsburgh Street to Pine Street was getting ready to be paved for the first time, and no longer would the boy have to run through what was commonly called "Yowler's Mortar Box" because of the muddy conditions. C.D. Yowler was the street foreman.

Moving about were horse-drawn buckboards and Model-T cars along the unpaved roads. There was the Muessers' Bread Truck delivering to Marshall and Rist Grocery fresh-baked goods. The town's lone mailman carried letters in a wheelbarrow that he pushed throughout the city. He stopped at the firehouse to deliver mail as the fire truck left, being pulled by hand. Blocks of ice came delivered from an ice truck.

The women's clothing concealed their legs above the calf, and there was undoubtedly no cleavage. The men were either in workers' clothes or simple sport coat and top hat attire. The boys wore baggy britches, and girls' dresses had slips underneath.

When John reached the main intersection of East Crawford Avenue and Brimstone Corner, he sprinted across it and headed to old Fayette Field.

Several years later, John Woodruff would enter Fayette Field with a banner above it reading: Connellsville High School, Class of 1925. Old Fayette Field was full of weeds without the soft rubber tartan track that today's athletes used, but this track was of dusty coal cinders. The runners dug the balls of their shoes into the cinders to get off on a fast sprinting start. Sprinting blocks used by today's athletes were not yet invented.

Young John ran around the track as his feet pounded and kicked up dust. It was here that the kid found inspiration, yearning to race like the wind someday in front of huge stadiums filled with rabid fans cheering him on.

As Johnny matured into his early teens, his legs began to strengthen with muscle like the cords of a sturdy rope. His stride kept extending, and his head still held high as if he was running at attention.

There were no coaches to train John, nor did he seem to need them. He kept busy competing against himself, his playmates—both real and imaginary—and his train arch-rival.

It was a hot summer day, and beads of sweat glistened on John's handsome but severe face. He looked like a sleek panther as his running now extended into farmland and the hillsides, legs working like pistons to meet the challenge of ascending the steep inclines.

Eventually, Johnny's run meandered back down to the railroad yards to again face his arch-rival, the locomotive. By now, its burly conductor knew when to expect John in the yard. Though the young boy continued to come in second to the train, the margin of victory became narrower.

John saw the train waiting for him, and his mind began forming the image. He could see himself at the starting line and being the first to cross the finish line.

The locomotive belched and steamed like a charging bull as it left the yard. John felt the train's power bearing down on him, but he was not intimidated. He kept his rhythmic form and let his long legs do the rest. However, the train beat John again, but this time narrowly. He waited to hear the engineer's inevitable loud whistle seemingly meant to mock him. But it did not come. The teen gazed up to see the engineer tipping his hat in respect to his foe.

It dawned on John that often out of periods of losing come the greatest stirrings toward a new winning streak. One learned from life's losses, and John knew his life would have its share of failures and learning.

In 1934, the high-school-aged face of John had matured, handsome and chiseled, carrying a solemn expression, while his legs became packed with more striated muscle. John's intake of air now came in deep, precise breaths. Added muscle on his frame, plus a mind forged in steel, worked to produce an unbelievably long stride, over nine feet—a good two feet longer than any of those running behind him. John was so far ahead of the pack that his new spiked running shoes kicked dust into the faces of his competitors as he dug deep into the dusty coal tracks.

John went back again to challenge the locomotive. The engineer cocked an eyebrow and gave a wave of recognition. By now, the conductor's once-stern expression had softened considerably. He had been won over by the determined kid who had never said a word to him. He knew what the kid was made out of, something he felt everyone should aspire to, including himself.

Their grudge match continued. The train burst out of the yard, angry and mean.

Two machines—locomotive and man—ran at an even clip. It was at this moment that John found another gear inside of him—character. He finally understood that racing against competition was all between the ears. His mind became trained to simply not accept the panic rising in him, trying to overtake him with insecurities. He simply focused on winning, never allowing himself to be complacent when coming in second place.

A blinding brightness filled his mind, and fire overtook his belly. His legs pushed him onward until Long John hit the "sweet spot" inside of him, that zone where feet sailed so fast that they seemed to be floating on air. His God-given speed and human tenacity had combined to outrace the train!

The engineer, expecting this day would eventually come, had an uncharacteristically broad grin. He honored the young champion by giving him a military salute followed by taking off the big red handkerchief from around his neck and waving it out the window. The engineer knew that inside of the boy's chest beat the heart of a champion.

CHAPTER 6

Connellsville, 2001

Back under the oak tree, the curious girl asked another question. "Weren't you afraid of racing so close to that train?"

"You bet I was," Old John answered. "It felt like that mass of locomotive iron was about to swallow me. So, I made sure to stay out of its way, but just facing it was sort of a victory in itself."

The revered man leaned toward the girl. "Tell you a secret: that day I knew I'd be terrific. Something in my heart told me."

The teen became riveted by the smooth voice of the elder man telling his story.

"No one knew at the time, but someday I would astound in what was considered by many track experts as the greatest run in Olympic history," John continued. "And under the watchful eye of Adolf Hitler, who wanted me to lose badly. But none of this would've happened if it weren't for my mom," he said, "I wouldn't have won the Olympic Gold Medal. You see, my parents weren't interested in athletics."

"Why not?" the teen asked. "If you ran today and won medals, you'd be on T.V. doing *Nike, Pepsi Cola,* and lots of other commercials."

"Probably," John agreed. "But in my time, it was a different story. I was born too soon. I could've possibly qualified for a great deal of money if I were born later, having won the Gold Medal. When I won, television wasn't yet in use. You see, my parents were old school. All they wanted me to do was stay in school to keep the truant officer off of them!"

John told of going out for football and staying with the team until the week before the first game. "Well, now they had players running sprints up and down the field, and of course, we didn't have the best facilities."

Old John pulled out from his envelope another photo, this one of him wearing a football uniform.

"That uniform is from the Stone Age!" his teen listener exclaimed with a chuckle. "And those baggy pants, your leather helmet with no facemask! I bet it hurt when you got hit in the face?"

"It did," John confirmed. "And the shoes we wore in football and track were made of kangaroo leather. When it was raining, it would soak up water, add weight to the shoes, and get very heavy."

With football practice ending at dusk, young Johnny was getting home too late to finish his chores. "So, the deal was—football would have to go if I got behind in my chores."

He told of Fred Snell, the long-time secretary of the Connellsville Recreation Board, and one of the nation's foremost authorities on track and field. "Fred saw me on a softball field playing first base and told the track and football coach that I might be a possibility for those sports. The track coach was also the line coach of the football team, Joseph Larew.

"How could you improve so much in one year?" the young listener asked the town's living legend. "I mean, like, it was as if some bolt of lightning hit you, and you became faster."

"I don't know where it came from," old John answered. "I guess it was nature. But that newfound burst of speed changed my life, that's for sure."

His listener asked Woodruff if he ran faster because he trained harder.

"No. I used the same ordinary training," John answered. "Our preparation in those days was fun. We had a lot of fun. Nobody in our time ran one hundred miles in a week; it was unheard of."

Woodruff said his running technique was not that classical. "I didn't have good control of my limbs, but I was *powerful*. I would explode from the start, let my long legs set the pace, and I'd run my competition into the ground."

Old John recalled, "But then things changed, and I was playing football. My coach was also the same in track. A real pusher, that Joe Larew. We called him "Pop.""

CHAPTER 7

Connellsville Football Field, 1932

Young Johnny was far ahead of his teammates in a race down the field.

Johnny's mother, Sarah, moved past the field carting baskets of laundry. She observed her son's impressive running ability before trudging onward.

That evening Johnny rushed home, late again, only to be met at the door by his perturbed mom.

"Football practice is getting you home too late for chore work," Sarah said, none-too-pleased. "You think firewood, coal, an' twigs walk in on their own in the house an' stack themselves?"

Johnny became sorrowful. "I know Ma, but I like sports . . . football and track."

"I can see that. So quit football an' keep up your track running which gets you home earlier."

Johnny was somewhat depressed. "Okay."

At track practice, Coach Pop was with his assistant observing Young Woodruff run faster than the others.

Pop assessed. "That kid runs like he's got a firecracker up his backside."

"He could win some races," the assistant added.

"More than some. Johnny's born to run."

Pop eventually took the long-legged Woodruff youth aside. "The way I see it, there's no reason why you can't be a great runner. You look funny, gangly, and all, but we'll work things out. Put your heart into it, and everything'll work okay."

Young Johnny nodded. "Okay, coach, if you think so."

It did not take long for Johnny Woodruff to run in events with confidence, winning with ease. Even after only a brief period of workouts, Johnny was winning half-mile and mile races in the school's dual meets. At the annual University of Pittsburgh high school event, he was entered for both distances, winning the mile though being second at 880. After that defeat, he would win them all.

"Now, we didn't have a standard field for the track team to practice on," John continued. "We ran our wind sprints on the field, and then we often ran from the high school to the cemetery—Hill Grove Cemetery—and back. It was a mile up and back. We didn't have a regular track at our school, just a dirt path around the football field."

Young John kept up with the team's quarterback, Ralph Marilla—a fast runner and also a sprinter on the track team.

CHAPTER 8

Connellsville, 2001

"Before anything happened with me in running track," John informed his eager listener. "I decided to drop out of school at age sixteen."

"What? Why?" The teen girl did not understand.

Old John's voice suddenly turned sad. "The Depression came and hit us all. There was very little money in our house. School and books would just have to wait. We needed to eat, so I figured I could find some kind of job, earn a little bit of money, and help out at home. Many of my white friends dropped out of school to work in the local factory and were bringing home nice paychecks. It was kind of a given that once you graduated from high school, you got positions at the glass factory or mills."

Elder John recalled applying for a job with the foreman, who shook his head in rejection.

"I was trying to help my family, but the factory said they didn't hire Negroes. I couldn't understand; all I wanted was a job like anyone else."

Old John told the young girl of then having to look for work in another direction. He went to a military recruiting station to talk to an army man in uniform.

"Being rejected by the military recruiter also ticked me off," John said in a huff. "I was offering to put my life on the line for my country but was shocked to hear the color of my skin wasn't good enough. You start to wonder if something is mixed up. Now they did say they had their quota. I didn't believe that, so I returned to school and the track team. It turned out, that's what saved me. Had that not happened, the world would've never known anything about me."

He remembered returning home from winning a race, and his mom was again loading baskets of laundered clothes onto a cart wagon for Young John to assist her.

"Ma, the sportswriters say my long stride is something very different, extraordinary."

"Well, you got your height from me," Sarah answered. "But those legs of yours sure do stretch like they belong to a giraffe!"

Back in the present, John recalled, "Some were saying I had the longest stride of any human. That made me feel, I don't know, 'different.' Before I graduated in '35, I owned the new state record, plus the national school mile record with a 4:23 winning time. In that same week, I also set the national record in the 880 yards. Yeah, my running took off like a meteor."

"I don't know where my newfound speed came from," Old John admitted to the girl.

"I guess it was nature. A *New York Herald* sportswriter wrote I was "the Negro wonder whose stride has to be seen to be believed.""

A long procession of cars snaked toward Connellsville Stadium; a crowd lined up outside.

Aged John went on, "Track experts and fans came far and wide to see for themselves. They started calling me nicknames, like the Black Shadow of Pittsburgh."

"Who gave you that name?"

"One very famous writer who gave a lot of people nicknames—Damon Runyon."

Elder John told that Runyon wrote famous Broadway stories such as *Guys and Dolls* and also *Little Miss Marker*. However he was mainly a reporter and sports columnist. He was also famous for many athletes' tags such as the boxers "The Cinderella Man" (Jim Braddock) and "The Manussa Maulter" (Jack Dempsey).

"Other nicknames came my way," Woodruff continued. *"Johnny the Antelope,* and *the Black Panther of Pittsburgh, Seven League Boots, the Dusky man from Smoky City,* but one name stuck, *'Long John.'"*

Arthur Daley, another sports columnist for *The Times,* wrote of Woodruff, "He was inexperienced and had more changes of gait and direction than a wild goat going up a mountainside!"

"As awkward as I was, I really could explode from the start setting the pace and having the competition eat my dust," the respected Woodruff recalled.

Though he had been running all his life, he was a relative newcomer to the competition. Woodruff's success story was an improbable one, a tale where this profoundly modest man's running abilities took him from tiny South Connellsville to Pittsburgh to Olympic fame in a year.

The young girl asked, "Do you think you would've still gone to college if it weren't for track?"

"No," Woodruff answered without hesitation. "As I said, we were poor. If it weren't for my ability to run, I wouldn't have become famous. Certainly, I wouldn't have gone to college; no one in my family ever did. I probably would've stayed in Connellsville and been a laborer. If that had been the case, instead of my feet running on the track made of coke dust, my back would've been picking up heavy loads of coke and coal just to make a living."

CHAPTER 9

Connellsville, 1932

Inside the simple, poor Connellsville dwelling of young Johnny Woodruff, he was alone with his mom, away from his many siblings.

"I got mixed feelings about Pitt, Ma."

Sarah understood. "I know you do. Things these days ain't for the blacks. But they'll change, they just have to."

"I got my work cut out. Not the running but having to work hard for that college degree."

"Now your daddy an' me didn't go beyond grade school. If that degree's what you want, then use your mind with the grit you put into your long legs to get 'em a-motorin.'"

Young Johnny made a vow. "If I don't graduate from college, I'm never returning home."

"Then you better get that degree, because my boy's no failure!"

Long John wiped a tear off his mom's cheek and hugged her.

"Whatever you do, son, wherever you go, my heart'll always be with you."

"I know that."

"What did your brothers and sisters think about you going to college?" the teen asked.

"Well, that was just unheard of because none of my siblings finished high school," Woodruff said. "My sister Margaret was very fond of me. She always had this thing about being a nurse. So, she took the GED to qualify so she could enter Harlem Hospital in New York City. Her specialty was working with terminal people, people who are dying. That's the type of people she worked with. Margaret did this for many years and worked hard until she got her certifications."

John visited her at work in the Harlem hospital, caring for terminally ill black patients not accepted at white hospitals.

"Margaret died of cancer when she was fifty-five," he lamented. "I know she's with God. A great person she was."

After graduation from high school, Coach Larew sent Woodruff to the regional, tri-state AAU championship meet to go up against senior half-milers. John ran exceptionally well and won in a personal best of 1.55:1 at 800 meters. They raised money to send him to the national Junior AAU meet in Nevada, where he finished very closely behind the winner, Howie Borck, a year older, in the 800 m—winning time—1.55:1!

The local press gushed over his potential, ". . . want to see Woodruff, new miler, doing his stuff. There is a thrill in seeing his beautiful stride." And, ". . . Woodruff astonishing scholastic followers with his sensational stepping . . . had he been pressed at all, he might have bested 4:20 (mile) . . ."

At a meet in Morgantown, West Virginia, he met Ohio State running star Jesse Owens, and they hit it off. Jesse would become a lifelong friend and an inspiration to Woodruff.

From there, things began happening very fast for John Youie Woodruff.

CHAPTER 10

Nuremberg, Germany, 1935

Around the same time Long John was talking to his mom, Adolf Hitler was addressing 200,000 faithful followers in Zeppelin Field at a vast Nazi Party Rally. It was surrealistic as 130 searchlights focused on him at the podium, now a seasoned, compelling speaker who gestured wildly, whipping his worshippers into a manic frenzy.

Hitler was triumphant, beyond belief. "We are strong and will get stronger! Our Aryan destiny is meant to rule the world, and we will!"

His tone was as much a threat as a promise. Hitler's intoxicating power would soon wreak havoc on the world.

Hitler at Nazi rally adulated by his supporters.

CHAPTER 11

Connellsville, 1934 – Hill Grove Cemetery

A few weeks later, in Connellsville, a devastated John was at a funeral with his siblings, his father, Silas, and many of the family's white friends.

The name on the Tombstone read: *Sarah Woodruff*

Before he left for college, John's mother died of a heart attack. He would always remember her as a great woman who worked hard for her family, and her absence tore a big, painful hole in young John.

CHAPTER 12

Connellsville, 2001

"It was 1935, and many universities were courting me due to my national interscholastic record for the mile I set as a senior," he admitted. "I was interested in Ohio State because Jesse Owens was there."

Jesse, known as the "Buckeye Bullet," won a record eight individual NCAA championships and tied the record for four gold medals. He equaled the world record for the one-hundred-yard dash and set world records in the long jump and low hurdles.

"However, there were some businesspeople in Connellsville who were also Pitt men, and they got me an athletic scholarship to the University of Pittsburgh. One was a dentist named Doctor "Buzz" Campbell, and for him, the sun rose and set over Pitt. He kept after me pretty good until I went to that university about fifty miles away."

John's disclosure prompted another question from his young listener. "So, the people of Connellsville liked you and helped you get into Pitt?"

"It wasn't a question of them liking me. We liked each other, plain and simple. The color of our skin had nothing to do with it. If it weren't for that scholarship my town got me, I couldn't have made it. I was the only one from my family to go to college."

With so few opportunities in Connellsville other than working in the factories, running was John Woodruff's ticket to do something with his life, and he told himself that he had to do it.

"Just getting to Pitt University was a trial by fire in itself. I didn't have enough money to transport myself. The sheriff in Connellsville had me driven to the Pittsburgh campus, and I had only twenty-five cents in my pocket."

Once John readied to leave for Pitt, he knew he had his work cut out for him.

"Where you scared?" the teen listener asked.

"Not of the running," he insisted. "That was as easy for me as breathing. But I knew I had to work hard for that degree. I knew I was in for the battle of my life. I was going into the great unknown without any of my friends with me. But I overcame my fear of the unknown. And so can you overcome your fears. Just trust in God's purpose for you."

CHAPTER 13

Pittsburgh, 1935

Long John Woodruff sat in the front seat of a Police car driven by a white policeman.

"Now Johnny, everyone knows you're a well-mannered, quiet kid, no trouble-maker," the young police driver said. "Tell me again, why that is?"

"Because I'm always too busy running."

The policeman gleefully slapped his knee. "Bingo! Let your runnin' make the noise. We in Connellsville wanna see yer long stride chew up the track. *Gobble, gobble!*"

Young John rolled his eyes.

The policeman was ecstatic. "Just wait 'til those big-city boys have to eat your dust!"

Pittsburgh Hill District

John got out of the ride with a lone beat-up suitcase. He looked warily at the YMCA at 2621 Centre Avenue in front of him. And many black people were milling about.

The four-story brick building with residential housing was known to locals as only "The Hill," the 1.4 square-mile clusters of neighborhoods perched above downtown Pittsburgh.

YMCA in Hill District, Pittsburgh – John's off campus home for four years while at Univ. of Pittsburgh.

Never had John seen so many blacks in one place, but it was where he was supposed to stay, the YMCA. Some Connellsville people helped in getting him a room there for which he was grateful. Also assisting him was Robert L. Vann, a black lawyer and editor in chief of the *Pittsburgh Courier*, one of the leading African-American newspapers in the country that published local and national editions. Long John lived at the "Y" for the next four years, where he got acquainted with bedbugs.

Young Woodruff soon found out that the city's first black district, this uptown neighborhood was a Mecca of arts and culture, with a strong sense of community. The Hill District became known by many names: Little Harlem, Little Haiti, and "the crossroads of the world."

The Hill was the home of immigrants from twenty-five countries and a national center for African-American sports, journalism, theater, commerce, and a jazz haven for artists.

And the Hill knew a thing or two about baseball. Also, at prominence at the time were the Pittsburgh Crawfords of the Negro National League baseball league. The crowds gathered around Satchel Paige, John Gibson, and Cool Papa Bell as if they were rock stars. Many baseball experts say these black players and others were as good or better than the likes of hitter Babe Ruth or pitching great Cy Young. And few begged to differ.

Jazz evolved and thrived in Hill District's many lively night clubs, dance ballrooms, theaters, and the Musicians Club. Jazz giants Earl Hines, Roy Eldridge, Erroll Garner, Kenny Clark, Art Blakey, Stanley Turrentine, Billy Eckstine, Mary Lou Williams, Ray Brown, George Benson, and many others learned and honed their talents on the Hill. With the vast array of world-class musicians who performed there at a myriad of famous clubs, The Hill was indeed a night for fun.

One evening John strolled around "The Hill" bustling with life. He peeked into a lively nightclub playing Jazz music. Hearing a lot of big band roaring orchestration, singing, and dapper-dressed patrons dancing and gyrating in rhythm, Long John was getting into the rhythm, snapping his fingers.

Coming from a small town, Pittsburgh was overwhelming for him. Its Hill District was one lively place for black folk. Famous entertainers flocked there like bees to honey. He became tempted to go into them because they seemed so magical, but he would not have known what to do, and he did not have any money.

A striking black girl in her early twenties entered the club with her girlfriends, sizing up John.

"You a long drop of water," she said in a voice that seemed to purr. "Comin' inside to dance with me . . . ease my thirst?"

"I can't tonight, Miss. Maybe some other time."

"Hope so. I don't want to have to go lookin' for you."

Her girlfriends giggled as John bypassed the nightclubs.

Young John said to himself, "She sure is a pretty one!"

He strolled back to his Y home, studying the rivers below were teeming with tugs and barges, steel mills still sending up flames through tall chimney stacks. Seeing that at the wee hours in the morning was why the air would be so thick, the next day, that streetlights often have to be kept on all day.

Hill District, early days.

Through the din visibility, here and there, one might see what Ernie Pyle, the Pulitzer Prize winning American journalist and war correspondent, wrote: "Pittsburgh is a place of hills, mountains, cliffs, and rivers, up and down, around and around, in betwixt, much better suited to goats than people!"

Adding to the view was pair of long funiculars—inclines—sliding up and down the steep face of Mount Washington, 800 feet in length and the oldest one in America.

Inside the track coach's office, Long John got to meet Coach Carl Olsen, in his fifties and a no-nonsense head track coach.

The Swedish Olsen handed over a five-dollar bill to John. "That'll cover your food for the week. With hamburgers a nickel and hot beef sandwiches twenty cents, you'll get by."

"Thanks, Coach."

"I got you a job helping clean the campus grounds. You'll receive breakfast and lunch at the cafeteria and can take home sandwiches for dinner."

Pittsburgh's smoky Steel Mills, mid-1930s.

John was appreciative. "Sounds good. Thanks."

Across the Atlantic, another King of the chessboard was moving fast but silently—Adolf Hitler. On February 26, 1935, the Nazi leader Adolf signed a secret decree authorizing the founding of the Reich Luftwaffe as the third German military service to join the Reich army and navy. In the same order, Hitler appointed Hermann Goering, a German air hero from World War I and high-ranking Nazi, as commander in chief of the new German air force.

The Versailles Treaty that ended World War I prohibited military aviation in Germany. However, a German civilian airline–Lufthansa–was founded in 1926 and provided flight training for the men who would later become Luftwaffe pilots. After coming to power in 1933, Nazi leader Adolf Hitler began to develop a state-of-the-art military air force secretly and appointed Goering as German air minister. During World War I, Goering commanded the celebrated air squadron in which the great German ace Manfred von Richthofen–"The Red Baron"–served. In

February 1935, Hitler formally organized the Luftwaffe as a significant step in his program of German rearmament.

The Luftwaffe was to be uncamouflaged step-by-step so as not to alarm foreign governments, and the size and composition of Luftwaffe units were to remain secret as before. However, in March 1935, Britain announced it was strengthening its Royal Air Force (RAF), and Hitler, not to be outdone, revealed his Luftwaffe, which was rapidly growing into a formidable air force.

CHAPTER 14

Connellsville, 2001

The teen girl listening to Old John in Connellsville Stadium stirred from her rapture to ask, "So you didn't have what athletes have today—special diets and supplements?"

"No. My diet for the day was whatever I could find to eat!"

"Maybe a healthier diet and some vitamin supplements, and you could've had more energy to run faster?" John was asked.

"Probably so," John answered. "But it was the same back then for everybody running. See, it was just a sign of the times. That's the way things were."

Old John continued his story.

CHAPTER 15

Connellsville, 2001

In the fall of 1935, Woodruff first came to the University of Pitt while the Depression was still going on. With Woodruff on hand, it was indeed a golden era for sports at Pitt, located in the Oakland section of the city. And just completed was the towering Cathedral of Learning building, forty-two stories and 535-feet high. It indeed was, for Woodruff, a beacon of learning.

To most students, this Late Gothic Revival cathedral, the centerpiece of the University of Pittsburgh and the second tallest educational building in the Western hemisphere, was a sight to behold.

John recalled, "That tower of the Cathedral of Learning was truly a beacon of hope for me. I kept staring at it like it was a shrine from God himself! My mind wanted to conquer things inside of that Cathedral of Learning."

"I hit the books like you wouldn't believe," John emphasized to the young track girl listening, leaning on his every word.

Woodruff told of how whites at this time perceived the black athlete—their physicality as having an "animalistic" nature and the implication that blacks were somehow intellectually inferior.

John added, "I always felt that there were wishers, and then there were those who realize one's wishes. Just as I did in track, I painted a picture in my mind of what I would like to do or be. And one of those images was me going up in front of the university and receiving my diploma. I cared so much about that image that I did all I could to make it happen."

Old John told how they used to pull the track athletes out of class on a Wednesday to go to an away track meet. "I wouldn't return to school until Monday the following week. I had to take my books with me because I had to study to keep up with my other classmates. After all, the professors didn't care about running. They were interested in me as a student to keep up with my classes and my classwork. So, I always traveled with my books."

While on campus, Woodruff cleaned up garbage in the stadium after football games and other events, and worked in the cafeteria. Those were his jobs to earn spending money.

At the time, television was only on the cusp of being invented. Airplanes had propellers. Model T cars, crank-started, had just been replaced by never designed vehicles. Telephones were of the crank-up kind often fixed on the wall. Cell phones were non-existent.

The youthful listener did not comprehend, asking, "Crank up phones? I don't understand how that works!"

CHAPTER 16

Pittsburgh, 1935

Inside John's room at the YMCA was sparse: two single beds, a wash-basin, two small desks, and the communal bathroom down the hall. John had a student roommate his age named Irvin, "Irzie." Early on at Pitt, John was ready to leave for class one day, but his roommate was still snoring.

"Irzie, get up!" John coaxed. "You can't keep missing classes."

A half-awake Irzie peered out the window. "Can't go today. Too much snow. 'Sides, that class starts too early."

John nudged him again. "C'mon. You're way behind in your studies."

When Irzie went back to snoring, John left.

They asked Irzie to leave Pitt after the first semester when he failed in his classes. John did not want that happening to him—an embarrassment to his community and family, so he studied like the dickens.

Later on in the day that he left Irzie, John was with a white student, Link Sardor, who helped him by reviewing his work before handing it in.

"You're getting the hang of it, John. These descriptions are much better."

"You think so?"

"Yeah. No one will confuse your essay with Shakespeare's, but it should get you a passing grade."

Several white students passed by them, shaking their heads and snickering, someone mumbling, *"Dumb Negro."*

An irritated Link stood up to them. "Hey! This guy has more natural smarts than you dimwits!"

The librarian hushed Link for talking so loud, the white student's leaving at the commotion.

"Don't get in trouble over me, Link."

"No trouble. I get pissed when hearing that blacks are as dumb as dirt. I want to let you know that I disagree. Just keep on proving them wrong."

John was all ears when it came to his English professor, lecturing. It was his weakest class of achievement, and he had to work double-time. John kept his nose in the books, but the English class was an ordeal. He had only learned Standard English before Pitt, and his professor was as tough as they came. John was to write an essay with an investigative theme and picked Ludwig van Beethoven. He put his heart and soul into it and used to lay on his cot at night thinking about the future, knowing he had to get this right. His buddy Link looked over his work and gave the thumbs up. But the professor said it was 'too general' and gave John a "D." He was happy just to have passed the hardest course at Pitt. After that, just like Link said, learning became more natural, and his grades started to improve.

John told his lone listener of enjoying the rest of his student days at Pitt. It was stimulating for him, and he had accomplished a lot of the goals that he set for him. Young Woodruff told of being an avid reader that went beyond those books required for his classes. After initially considering Majoring in Physical Education, he decided to Major in Sociology at Pitt. He liked people and was curious about how they lived in other parts of the world.

Running was a different story. When it came to track, Long John was on the Dean's List. No matter what distance the race, long-legged John out-stretched all competition.

Coach Olsen said in amazement to Long John, "Of all the half-milers at Pitt, you can beat 'em all."

"Excuse me, coach, isn't that the point?" John answered in question.

"I know, you're a natural talent if I ever saw one. Now I want you to go against our 100-yard sprint men."

"That's not my event."

"Just want to see what's inside that engine of yours," Olsen said with a competitive grin.

John did as he was told and tied Pitt's top champion at the finish line.

"We got us a Jesse Owens here!" shouted Olsen with glee.

An assistant coach looked at his stopwatch time. "Or a Jim Thorpe. The kid's born to run, and he's only a freshman!"

The idea of Long John running different distance races, and winning, had Olsen salivating.

"Catch your breath, Johnny," the coach said with encouragement. "Next . . .take on our milers."

Pitt's top miler looked to Coach, shaking his head. "That's okay, coach. Don't want it going around that a freshman beat me!"

Long John raced against all white runners at Army at West Point, New York, and easily defeated them.

Some white fans begin taunting him with catcalls, boos, and slanderous names.

A spectator yelled out: "Go back to the jungle with your monkey and ape relatives!"

"Nigger go home!"

A part of John wanted to rip into those guys, but he kept his cool when unpleasant things like that happened. He did not want to give Pitt a bad name, or maybe even lose his scholarship. At times, things seemed to be working out, but now and then, Jim Crow would rear its ugly head.

Woodruff's white running teammate Don Ohl gestured in anger to a bigoted rowdy group before saying to John, "Don't mind those asshole jerks!"

John got off the team bus in a following away meet that had a couple of black athletes, and he scanned a book they carried called *The Negro Travelers' Green Book*. The Green Book was a Bible of sorts for every Negro traveler during John's early days. Black folk did not dare leave home without it. It provided a rundown of hotels, guest houses, service stations, drug stores, taverns, and restaurants that were known to be safe destinations for African American travelers.

"Well, guys," Long John brought up, "where do we lay down our heads tonight?"

"If we don't find any hotels for our kind," a teammate answered, "I got the name of a family that might take us in."

John and his black teammates entered a seedy place that had the sign announcing: *Adams Hotel, Negroes Welcomed*

Inside their room, the lights were out, and the athlete alongside John slept, but John used a flashlight so he could study from a textbook.

No matter how tired he was, many of his nights were spent studying. He used to envy his roommates when they just fell asleep with no cares, but John had homework to do. Besides running on the field, he felt he was running for his life.

Long John was back on the track field at Pitt practicing with his white running teammates, running in dual meets, and sometimes arguing with Coach Olsen.

Long John winning one of many races for University of Pittsburgh. (Courtesy of University of Pittsburgh.)

He and his coach mostly got along. He was very ambitious, always trying to get the ultimate out of John. But he also leaned toward making him run too much, sometimes in four events: the 220, 440, 880, and the mile. John did not mind it so much in dual meets, but Coach always wanted more.

Olsen remained dogged. "I believe you also have what it takes to be a hurdler."

"Coach, I just finished running all these races and tackling the 800-meter. I get plenty tired just running on flat ground, without jumpin' over something!"

An irritated Olsen walked away in a huff.

The runners on John's relay team laughed over his answer.

"If 'Little Napoleon' Olsen had his way," Don Ohl quipped to John, "he'd have you pulling the team bus to our meets!"

The teammates walked off, still chuckling.

CHAPTER 17

Pittsburgh, 1935

In History Class at Pitt, John listened to a professor lecture on Germany. A slide show projector froze on a photo of Adolf Hitler.
On the chalkboard was written:

January 30, 1933, Hitler appointed Chancellor of Germany
February 28, 1933, Suspension of freedoms of speech, assembly,
    press, and other fundamental rights
March 20, 1933, First concentration camp opens at Dachau
April 1, 1933, Nazi-organized boycott of Jewish-owned
    businesses
April 7, 1933, Jews excluded from government employment,
    including teaching jobs at all levels
July 14, 1933, New law provides the basis for forced
    sterilization of disabled persons, Gypsies, and Blacks
October 1934, The first significant wave of arrests of
    homosexuals throughout Germany
March 16, 1935, Military conscription introduced
April 1935, Many of Jehovah's Witnesses arrested throughout
    Germany
September 15, 1935, Anti-Jewish racial and citizenship laws
    issued at Nuremberg

The professor continued, "As you can see, there's a pattern in Hitler's behavior."

John continued to listen to the lecture while sketching a figure in his notebook. It was of the mustached Adolf Hitler.

Old John lamented under the Woodruff Tree to his youthful listener, "I had no idea at the time that Hitler and I would be linked forever in history."

CHAPTER 18

Rhine, Germany Countryside, 1935 – One Year Before the '36 Olympics

Nazis retaliated against the black African soldiers brought into the Rhine and some of their families.

A Nazi officer barked to a subordinate soldier, "Round up these Rhineland bastards!"

The black Germans were corralled, mistreated, and forced into trucks.

"To be taken where sir?" asked the subordinate.

"We're to put them in camps for sterilization," the officer divulged. "The Reich doesn't want *Mischlings* polluting the Motherland."

"What then with these mulattos, *Mein Herr?*"

"Until the Olympics are over, hard labor camps. After that . . ."

Office of Reich Chancellor, 1935

Adolf Hitler paced around a table seating the leading cabinet Reich members. "Our Olympic Games will be the greatest ever," he extolled with confidence. "But we need the U.S. to pull it off. If they participate, other countries will follow. The problem is what to do about the Jews?"

Joseph Goebbels, in his forties, a short, gaunt, cadaverously thin scarecrow, and the Minister of Propaganda spoke up, saying, "The international community won't participate in our Games until assured Nazi Germany treats Jewish sportsmen as well, correct?"

"Yes," Hitler answered. "And they'll boycott unless we include them on our team. That's the big problem needing overcome."

Goebbels had a ready answer. "*Mein Fuhrer*, what if we call upon the Jewish sports federations to nominate a representative for our team?"

Hitler became intrigued. "So, we take one "token" Jew?"

"Correct."

"A small price to pay for America to come to Berlin?"

"Precisely," assured Goebbels. "And we know of a particular half-Jewish athlete."

Hitler became excited over the ruse. "If the Yanks come, other countries will follow, giving Germany its victory!"

Goebbels painted for his lead an even bigger picture. "We'll call the Games the "Nazi Olympics.""

"Brilliant!" Hitler was beyond ecstatic.

Goebbels added, "A big propaganda display will demonstrate the superiority of our Master Race."

Hitler became bright-eyed with the craze. "We have our solution!"

Reich members congratulated one another for their master plan. Even Jews from Hitler's Germany had fallen victim. Hitler's word of honor meant nothing.

A year earlier, the Olympic decision-makers, men keeping a watchful eye on Hitler, approached him. One was the International Olympic Committee president Henri de Baillet-Latour.

"You must give your word," Henri said sternly to Hitler, "that the Berlin Olympics will be free of racial discrimination. And that pledge means Jewish athletes will be part of the German team."

An appalled Hitler gave his answer to the IOC president. "When one invites you to a friend's home, you don't tell him how to run it, do you?"

Baillet-Latour's response was quick and to the point. "Excuse me, Mr. Chancellor, when the five rings are raised over the stadium, it is no longer Germany. It is the Olympics, and we are masters here."

Hitler was beside himself, on the verge of going into one of his classic rages. Yet he controlled himself.

"You will be satisfied," he snorted before storming out of the room with his subordinates in tow.

This standoff could be the only time that Hitler's Nazis would ever back down from anyone, except an army. He would even put two half-Jews on the German team, fencer Helen Mayer, and Rudi Ball, the hockey star.

For the clever, devious mind of Hitler, this would be the only conceal-ment, a token gesture to mollify the West. No other Jewish athlete would compete for Germany. Mayer would claim a silver medal in women's foil and, like the other medalists for Germany, would give the Nazi salute at the podium.

CHAPTER 19

Franklin Field, Philadelphia, 1936

The largest two-tiered stadium in the country at the University of Pennsylvania and home of the Army-Navy football game became packed with over 40,000 track fans. Pitt's 880 sprint relay team had John Woodruff, Dick Ohl, Al Ferrara, and Dick Mason running far ahead of opponents.

The scoreboard displayed: *3:34.5 – New World Record*

Inside the locker room after the meet, Coach Olson motioned to John to come into his office.

Coach got right to the point. "I know you're only a novice, but you should try out for the Olympic team."

Long John became hesitant. "I don't know. What makes you think I can run with those veterans?"

"Because I know talent when I see it."

"What'll I have to do?" the prized athlete asked.

"It's very simple," Olsen said with a wry smile. "Run like the wind!"

John Woodruff began traveling in a station wagon rambling along the highway to races at various track meets just before the '36 Olympics. Giving him added support were his Connellsville boosters going with him: Pop Larew, along with his good friend, Orell (Rube) Herwick—a great all-around sportsman. Also, with them was ex-railroader Fred Snell,

JOHN WOODRUFF IS ONE OF THREE MEN IN THE HISTORY OF THE NCAA DI OUTDOOR TRACK & FIELD CHAMPIONSHIPS TO WIN THREE CONSECUTIVE HALF-MILE TITLES. HE WAS UNDEFEATED AS A COLLEGIAN AND WON THE 1939 CROWN BY ONE FULL SECOND.

That doesn't even mention that he was UNDEFEATED at everything from the 400/440 to the 800/880 in collegiate competition (USTFCCA – U.S. Track and Field and Cross Country Coaches Assoc.)

another great all-around sportsman who was keeping records of Woodruff's feats for a scrapbook.

Woodruff moved up the ladder during the elimination contests, starting with the Allegheny Mountain Association Meet 880, then on to Lincoln, Nebraska. The semi-finals at Harvard capped off by the New York City finals.

As Long John won yet again and flashbulbs popped, Snell quipped, "I'm going to need a bigger scrapbook to keep up with Johnny!"

But even before they traveled to those qualifying meets, Pop Larew said in a speech to the Connellsville Rotary Club, "John Woodruff will not only gain an Olympic berth, but he'll win the 800-meter race in the Olympics." Now, how's that for a prediction?

Olsen drove John up to New York City's Randalls Island in the borough of Manhattan in the Harlem River for the finals, a race that would decide which American track players would go to the Olympics.

Old John's mind was still razor-sharp. "It had been scorching and humid as we drove up to New York in Coach's car. With him and me were Pitt's athletic director and also a black sprinter on the team, a guy named Mason. He didn't make the team, missing a team place by one yard."

The quiet, retiring Woodruff told of the athletes he raced against in New York City that day. It had been a standout field of nationally acclaimed American distance runners like Ben Eastman of California, whom some track experts called invincible, Chuck Hornbostel and Marmaduke Hobbs of Indiana, Harry Williamson of North Carolina, Charley Beethman of Ohio State, Abe Rosenkrantz of Michigan Normal, and Jimmy Miller of UCLA.

"Coach kept pushing me hard; he trusted me more than I did myself. Somehow he knew I could do it."

John's strong running had Pittsburgher's talking about this wondrous athlete. They spoke of natural athletes that stood out from all the rest, which made things look so easy that they hardly seemed to sweat while performing. Among all the great athletes, the long, fluid, and powerful running stride of John Woodruff ranked with the best.

"I might have put Connellsville on the map," he told his teen listener. "But back then, nobody heard about Connellsville. The people at Pitt and the colleges I ran against asked me, 'Where you from?' And I eventually began telling them the Pittsburgh area because I knew they knew where Pittsburgh was, and if I'd said Connellsville, they wouldn't know where that was. Yeah, a little hick town."

CHAPTER 20

Randall's Island, New York City, July 11-12, 1936 – Final Track and Field Events to Choose Olympic Team

Long John was at the starting line against his opposing runners. Some sportswriters were saying that despite his long stride, Woodruff did not have even a dark horse's chance of breaking the tape ahead of Eastman.

Meanwhile, back in Connellsville, John Woodruff was the talk of the town. "All Johnny's gotta do is win the Olympic trail finals, or finish second, and he's headed for Germany!"

A newspaper article described that blistering hot day of July 12, 1936—the day of decision for Johnny Woodruff. Connellsville captured the mood as the whole town awaited the news if Johnny would be an Olympian. It was just as sportswriter Kriek would later describe it.

The Fayette County residents were sitting on their porches fanning themselves while drinking iced tea, hoping the predicted rainstorms and high wind would bring some relief from the drought. The thermometer reached 100.

They had their radios on awaiting the news since television had only become invented.

Even at the old Fighting 10th regiment of the Spanish-American War that was getting ready for a reunion at nearby Mt. Pleasant, everyone was sitting by their radios to hear about the "big race" in New York City.

At the newly built Downing Stadium on Randall's Island, a stone's throw in clear eyesight from Manhattan, what President Franklin D. Roosevelt saw with the thousands of other spectators in attendance was incredible. The starter sounded the gun and sent the field away. After Woodruff trailed Eastman almost all around the track, the heron-legged Pitt freshman suddenly stretched out his incredible length of a limb in a space-eating stride that one reporter called a "never-never land stride."

Long John, in warp speed, quickly went through in his mind the science behind an 800-meter race. He knew that there was no magic mileage figure that would guarantee success. A half-mile runner had to make decisions and respond to events in their race in a split second. Even a moment's hesitation could make the difference between winning and losing. Not to mention the 800 being a tightly-bunched race, one that its runners were used to running in traffic. And there was the biggest challenge facing an 800-meter runner—avoiding interruptions in pace. To avoid all that, Long John usually liked to get out front of the pack and stay there to the very end.

Track experts were calling world record holder Ben Eastman of Stanford invincible. But his record did not mean much to John, whose only goal was to win. As soon as that starter gun went off, nothing ever distracted him.

Long John, head held back high and proud, legs stretching beyond belief, beat Eastman with ease.

John missed topping his 800-meter world record by just one-tenth of a second. John's support group ran up to congratulate him.

"If Eastman would've given me stiffer competition," young Woodruff shared with them, "I feel I might've broken his world record."

Pop was beside himself. "Johnny! You're going to the Olympics!"

Young Woodruff pinched himself. A small-town kid was going to Germany! It all happened so fast.

Johnny had not just become the instant hero of Connellsville, but other cities across America picked up on this quiet, athletic young man. Everyone who had witnessed Woodruff run in those two races was aghast. The articles about Woodruff were flowing.

"Woodruff has the longest stride I've seen on a human being," said Nate Cartnell, former Olympic coach. "Chuck Hornbostel is no mincing stepper, but the Hoosier was taking three strides to Woodruff's one as they came down the home stretch in the final tryouts."

Cartnell continued in the vaguely racist style of those times, "Woodruff's form violates all the copybook rules, but who cares for style when a fellow has a stride like that darky's. No wonder Eastman, off to a bad start, got discouraged chasing that black panther."

"Woodruff is the most unorthodox and spectacular strider I've ever seen," asserted Tom Keane, the Syracuse coach who was disappointed by the failure of his protégé Eddie O'Brien to survive the tryouts. "Woodruff is as unorthodox as Jesse Owens is smooth."

A *New York Times* reporter, who described Woodruff as an "unheralded Negro freshman from the University of Pittsburgh," gave this account of the race against Hornbostel: "Woodruff steps along with gigantic strides, his head pulled back as though he were trying to kick it with his heels. His form is terrible, but his running superb. He matched the great Chuck Hornbostel's kick with a sprint of his own, opened up a 3-yard lead in the final 20, and triumphed in the grand time of 1:51.3. The Pitt Negro looks bad enough winning, but when he was losing, he seemed very much through for the day. Just as the 'experts' started to write the name of Hornbostel down in their programs as the inevitable winner, the Negro reversed the Louis-Schmeling procedure and flattened the Hoosier with one blow. He streaked away from Hornbostel and won so handily that mental notes were made immediately to reserve a place for him on the Olympic team."

Amazingly, Eastman, the guy who held the world record, did not even make the Olympic team. Some said he was not used to the hot and humid weather, but hot weather didn't bother John. He liked it. The hotter the better.

The articles about Woodruff were again hot off the press.

One city was Philadelphia nearly three hundred miles from Connellsville.

The Philadelphia Courier wrote: "Johnny Woodruff is not only a hero to the folks of Connellsville, but he has been taken into the hearts of all, regardless of where they live."

Another article from back home in Pittsburgh's Hill District said the Negroes there were enthusiastically planning a mammoth celebration for their new hero upon his return from the Olympics. They were ready to turn out only as the high-energy Hill District could pridefully.

CHAPTER 21

Connellsville, 2001

"What happened next?" asked the attentive listener under the Wood-ruff Tree, John's only audience.

"The Olympics committee assigned me a uniform," John remembered.

He described it being a dark Olympic blazer, trousers, and a white straw hat that all the Olympians would wear.

Old John told that as a college freshman, he was along with hundreds of other athletes representing the United States. The tall, handsome, rock-hard runner had stayed in New York's Lincoln Hotel in the Times Square area as the Olympic team assembled. Being in hustling and bustling Manhattan was fascinating for this small-town young man, as was this voyage on the big ship, the most fantastic time in John's life. He was representing the US in the Berlin Olympics 800-meter (half-mile) race yet had never been on a boat or this far away from home.

John also told that the appreciative citizens of Connellsville sent him 115 dollars in spending money before he left for Berlin. He added, "You have no idea how much their kindness meant to me."

Under the Woodruff Oak in Connellsville, the venerable Woodruff's gentle but descriptive storytelling continued to rivet his audience of one.

"On that ship, I felt my mom and many town-folk sailing with me."

"Weren't you nervous?" the girl asked. "I mean, going to face the best runners in the world?"

"Nervous, but not so much because of running," Woodruff answered. "There were more serious matters, like racial tension and politics."

Old John would never forget that wondrous voyage, his first. "Watching all the athletes working hard on their specialty brought us together. Most of us didn't know each other much. We were experiencing a long journey for the first time. Given this situation, you might think relations were awkward, but we bonded quickly and even maintained friendships long after the Olympics were over. Eighteen black track athletes and seven Jews . . . we had no idea that we were about to shake the world."

The men and women athletes did their jumping jacks, holding each other's ankles while doing sit-ups, jogging in place, lifting Indian clubs, and tossing to each other the heavy medicine ball.

"These athletes going over to Berlin were a breath of fresh air," Old John never forgot. "Though they were serious about their events, they weren't bogged down by "the business of the Olympics," as today's athletes are. Carrying that American flag, being part of the best that America had to offer, that was what the Games were about to these women and men."

Not to be found aboard the deck was any advanced equipment or personal trainers, private physicians, or their marketing agents that star athletes of today would have on this trip.

———

Sailing to Germany, July 1936

Newspaper Headlines: The Ship-Ride to Germany and a Rumor of War

Another Headline: On to Berlin—the USS *Manhattan* Sails with Olympians. Thousands Cheer Them Off

On July 15th, 1936, leaving New York City harbor and setting sail for Germany was the country's largest and potentially strongest American Olympic team in history. They were aboard gaily be-flagged SS *Manhattan* in a clamor of bon-voyage cheers from more than ten thousand well-wishers and ear-splitting din from the tied-down whistles of harbor craft. Thousands on both the New Jersey and New York sides of New York

Harbor lined docks, parks, the street ends, and anyplace they could see the ship pass. American flags waved from spectators cheering on the athletes.

The crowd chanted in rhythm, "Ray! Ray! For the USA! Hooray!"

The vessel was the flagship of the United States Lines—the first in the company's fleet constructed exclusively for passengers. The SS *Manhattan* was 705-feet long and eighty-six-feet wide, cruising at a speed of 20 knots. Typical transatlantic crossings would find the ship carrying six hundred or more passengers and a crew of five hundred. On this trip, though, it was packed with nearly four hundred Olympic athletes, managers, and another eight hundred and fifty passengers, mostly family, friends, the press, and members of the American Olympic Committee (AOC); they filled the three classes of accommodations.

There was a fever-pitch excitement onboard. Avery Brundage, the President of the United States Olympic Committee, made a rousing speech to the media: ". . . Thanks to the patriotic sportsman of America, we're off to Berlin with the largest and finest team we've ever sent abroad . . ."

It was probably the grandest and noisiest farewell New York had yet seen. Ashore and afloat, and even in the air—where airplanes and blimps soared and dipped—exuberance was so manifest, it almost knocked one's hat off. It was a tornado of massed joy because the team was off to the games—"full strength"—after weeks of apprehensive uncertainty over financial shortages and also political problems.

Onboard, Young Woodruff joined the most famous black American athlete of them all, twenty-three-year-old Jesse Owens—a short but tremendously athletic and graceful runner.

They observed a burly athlete with sea sickness throwing up overboard.

Jesse chuckled. "That big shot putter is giving his best tosses overboard!"

"I'm okay," Woodruff made known, "but I never knew there was so much water on the planet."

However, not all the athletes were exercising on the port side and starboard areas or taking photos. The choppy Atlantic waters gave much onboard motion sickness. On their second night out at sea, they hit a wild and pitching storm that rocked the boat to no end. The retching, moaning, and the claustrophobia of being below in a small cabin had become a sort of hell. Stepping foot on land once again had become as much a goal as winning an Olympic Gold medal.

Seasickness had overtaken quite a few of the athletes on the SS *Manhattan*. Many stayed below most of the trip. Not only would they have to work quickly to get back into track shape, but they would also, like the rest of the athletes, have to get their land legs back.

"You nervous, Jess?"

"Not really, I can't wait to give those Nazis a whoopin'."

Woodruff nodded in agreement. "Hitler thinks we're 'inferior non-humans.'"

"So? Many in America feel the same."

"I won't let that get to me," Young John assured.

"Then let's make sauerkraut outta German runners and all others!"

As Woodruff and Owens bonded, they observed other athletes captured on film for posterity. There were the weight-men, led by weightlifter Anthony Terlazzo, discus thrower Ken Carpenter, and decathlon star Glenn Morris. On the swimming and diving team were swimmers Jack Medica, Adolf Keifer, and Eleanor Holm Jarrett, and the divers Richard Degener and Marshall Wayne. There also was the great and famous runner Glen Cunningham.

"Hey, guys!" a wiry-built white runner jogging by yelled out to the two black athletes.

"Hey, Louie Z!" shouted Young Woodruff. "I hope to race you someday in the mile!"

"Now that would be a great race!" Louie said with a smile before continuing.

"Who's that?" asked Jesse.

"Louis Zamperini, the 5000-meter distance runner from California," John answered. "He's the only guy during my high school senior year that ran a faster mile than me. Had I known someone would beat my record by two seconds, I would've turned on the gas some more!"

No one knew at the time that Zamerpini would be a famed World War Two veteran and become a Japanese Prisoner of War survivor whose story would turn into a lavish Hollywood film in 2014, *Unbroken,* directed by actress Angelina Jolie.

Off in another corner, practicing hoops on a make-shift basket was the American basketball team. These upcoming Olympics would mark the first time that basketball would become a sport as well as soccer, handball, canoe/kayak, and water polo.

In another section, boxers hit the heavy and speedy bags while others shadowboxed and skipped rope. Two fighters were sparring while wearing headgear.

Nineteen sports, 129 events, and 4,069 athletes from forty-nine countries, more than any previous Olympics, would compete in events from August 1st to the 16th.

The longer John and Jesse Owens talked, the more they became aware of how highly combustible the world was at this time. By the two athletes sharing their concerns, the weight of their burdens seemed to lessen. And that was true. Down South, segregation was a fact of life in America at this time. America was white, and that is that. Blacks became barred from white schools, hotels, restaurants, parks, and beaches. Blacks were sitting in the "colored" carriages of trains and at the rear of buses. No matter how you cut it, blacks were second class citizens in most everything.

However, Jesse Owens and John Woodruff were attending white universities and were on a mission.

As the Olympics approached, most blacks eagerly anticipated the opportunity to show up the Nazis while exposing Jim Crow racism in America.

John nodded that he understood. Like many of the black athletes of the day, tensions were about to become quite high at the Berlin Games.

The two exceptional athletes limbered up before a run.

Onboard the cruise liner, journalists, photographers, and documentary filmmakers milled about. Woodruff, Owens, and other athletes began posing for the media in various forms of activity. Jesse and John wore

USA Olympic uniforms as they lined up for them in a mock race, while various Olympians were on board, including women doing calisthenics in baggy warm-up suits.

After working out, white and black athletes, male and female, dressed in formal evening wear and posed for photos. However, there was one female athlete aboard the SS *Manhattan* having too much of a good time.

A young female athlete was having a perfect time at the bar. Eleanor Holm Jarret was a 22-year old swimmer from Brooklyn whom they said: "trained on champagne and cigarettes." However, she was a great swimmer, having already swum in the Olympics and, four years previously, had slashed three seconds from the world record while winning Gold in the 100-meter backstroke. Some said she was so fast in the water that she did not even get wet!

She was at the bar with a group mostly comprised of men. Among them were the leading sportswriters on the SS *Manhattan*—Paul Galico, Alan Gould, and Joe Williams, who loved her company. Eleanor told jokes, flirted, drank champagne, and sang songs.

The swimmer was also friends with Clark Gable and took acting lessons with his wife.

It was as she was ready to leave that party, Olympic Committee chief, Avery Brundage, saw her and reprimanded her for her "non-Olympic" behavior. Eleanor took him lightly, "Slavery Avery," who cracks the whip turned out to be a big mistake.

One of the women chaperones observed Eleanor staggering back to her cabin. The team doctor and the ship's physician was called in to examine her. As everyone already knew, she became smashed on champagne.

In Jarret's cabin, she sobbed to Brundage, begging, "I swear I'll never touch another drop!"

Brundage was not buying it. He was bent on removing any athlete who questioned his autocratic rule.

Eleanor Jarrett was gone from the Olympics.

Sitting in the deck lounge area, having a drink with his subordinate assistant was Avery Brundage. The forty-nine-year-old construction

John Woodruff (center) on the ship ride to Berlin. (Courtesy of University of Pittsburgh.)

mogul was the calculating, domineering US Olympic Committee Chairman. An army of reporters was interviewing him. After he finished their questions about Eleanor Jarret, talk went to another topic on everyone's mind.

"Well, there's a reason why the International Olympic Committee awarded these summer games to Berlin," Brundage told them. "A signal for Germany to return to the world community."

One of the reporters was the blunt Sam Rubenstein, in his late thirties. He said pointedly to Brundage, "Some are saying that's wishful thinking. That on your Berlin visit two years ago, they seduced you."

"Pure nonsense," countered Brundage. "I know what I saw."

"Many, including me, disagree with you. The Games shouldn't be in Berlin. Hitler's already turned the nation into a one-party dictatorship."

Brundage waved off the comment. "The Olympic Games belong to the athletes, not to the politicians."

Rubenstein did not back off. "Really? How come Hitler's excluding German Jews?"

Brundage was getting irritated. "You guys are jumping the gun. They have several performing, and our Jewish athletes are here."

Another reporter chimed in, "Only after much pressure put on the Reich. What's the matter? Can't you hear the distant war drums?"

Brundage kept his stance. "Germany learned its lesson. There won't be trouble."

Avery Brundage, US Olympic Committee Chairman.

But so did Rubenstein. "Mister Brundage, several Israeli newspapers are calling you anti-Semite. That you pay little attention to the prejudices against Jewish sports stars?"

Brundage looked at the name tag the reporter wore. "Sam Rubenstein of the Globe. Jewish?"

Rubenstein nodded. "One hundred percent."

Brundage signaled his Subordinate Assistant to write down the reporter's name. "Another of your race singling me out. Get in line behind the blacks!"

"I don't have to," Rubenstein countered. "You just gave me your answer, sir. Thank you."

Brundage, bristling, nodded to his subordinate, and they got up to leave. "Now if you'll excuse me, I've got work to do."

After he departed, the reporters talked amongst themselves.

"Why's he turning a blind eye?" a different reporter asked.

Rubenstein had a ready answer. "Because "Slavery Avery" is a rich, pompous racist!"

Another reporter also became outspoken. "He's been called other things, none too nice."

CHAPTER 22

German Chancellery, Berlin, Germany, July 1936

As Hitler sat in counsel, a knock sounded on the door. A note became handed to an assistant, who rushed it to Minister of Propaganda Goebbels to read. As his eyes scanned, he gave a sly smile.

"*Mein Fuhrer*, our disinformation campaign has worked splendidly! The American ship is too far out at sea to boycott the games and turn back."

Hitler was pleased. "Splendid. Let's treat our first Jew to the 'unfortunate' news."

Goebbels nodded. "Allow me the honor, *Mein* Fuhrer."

CHAPTER 23

Sailing to Germany on the USS *Manhattan, July 1936*

A group of Black athletes huddled with Long John and Jesse Owens in a Third-Class Section room below the waterline.

Ralph Metcalf, the twenty-seven-year-old veteran sprinter, and thoughtful spokesman among the black athletes, looked about the group. "Where's Howell?"

"Last I saw," a black athlete said, "he was with his coach."

"We'll start without him," Metcalf said. "Remember at all times we'll be watched by the whole world, so no matter what happens, we have to set an example. Let's show up the Germans!"

Jesse Owens spoke up, "Negro newspapers are callin' us the *Black Eagles*! We've become instant heroes."

"But we're nothing 'til we win gold," Metcalf reminded. "Don't forget that."

The group cheered, giving the war cry, *"Gold, gold, gold!"*

Metcalf kept them stoked. "Collecting Gold is our mission. So, let's do it!"

As the cheering continued, laughter intermingled, the athletes chanted their war cry.

A radio was flipped on, and jazz music sent the athletes into a frenzy, both men and women dancing with energy.

There was a pounding on the door. It was a white Jewish sprinter named Marty Glickman. The nineteen-year-old was a likable and comical fast-talking New Yorker with a wide-mouth grin.

"What's this? Throwing a party without me? Who has the latest Big Apple dance steps?"

A black athlete said in rebuttal, "We're born with the latest steps. Watch this!"

He did some fancy dance steps.

To Glickman, he said, "Where you from, man? You talk funny."

"The Bronx," answered Glickman. "God's country! Where they talk fast and dance faster."

The two got into an array of dance combinations. The rest jumped right into the boogie action. The singing and dancing were going full bore until the black boxer Howell King opened the door, a muscular young man with a piercing glare. He was in his early twenties and an irritable mood.

Metcalf shouted over the music, "Where you been, Howell?"

When Howell punched the door, the music stopped. "I'm bein' sent back home once we dock in Germany!"

Jesse was miffed. "Why? What's going on? Didya injure yourself?"

This time Howell punched the wall, his knuckles drawing blood. "Hell no! I'm bein' replaced. Coaches say I'm 'homesick.' What the hell's that mean? I didn't ride on no boat for ten days only to go right back to Detroit!"

"I don't get it," Jesse continued. "Maybe it's all a misunderstanding."

"A setup, man!" Howell seethed. "They say homesickness can't make me box good enough now, so a white fighter's gonna replace me."

"Sons of bitches!" Jesse Owens said. "They can't do that!"

"Homesick, my ass! I've been whupping sparring partners on this boat ride ever' day—black an' white both. Worked too damn hard to have this lyin' shit happenin' to me!"

"I agree with Jesse," Metcalf threw in. "They can't do this."

"Doncha, get it?" Howell asked the group. "They allow blacks to come, but then stop us from competing. Whose head is next to be on the chopping block?"

Tidye Pickett (back row, far right) and Louise Stokes (back row, third from the left) traveled to the Olympics with their team but were not allowed to compete. Tidye hurting her ankle going over a hurdle, while Louise Stokes was suddenly replaced in the 400-meter relay by a white runner because of her race. (Black History- black-women-in-sports)

Howell left in a huff, slamming the door behind him.

The two female athletes, Louise Stokes and Tidye Picket, both in their early twenties, looked to one another.

Louise spoke up. "They *can* do it; Lord knows they can. They pulled the same stuff on Tidye an' me in Los Angeles at the '32 Olympics." Tidye nodded. "Yanked us the last minute from the relay team, replaced by two white runners."

The athletes looked to Glickman, who said, "Hey, I may be white, but to the Nazis, I'm a low scum Jew!"

The following morning, Long John and Jesse Owens were working out together again.

Young Woodruff appeared troubled. "I couldn't sleep much, just *thinking* of Howell."

Marty Glickman and Sam Stoller sprint running champions who were not allowed to compete in Berlin Olympics because being Jewish.

"Same here. Hey, we can't get down in the dumps right now. Gotta keep our spirits up . . ."

"I hear ya," Long John agreed. "But I can't help thinking who might get pulled out next? Gotta keep my nose to the grind and run. You too, Jess."

They were interrupted by two other runners, the fast-talking Marty Glickman with the quietly thoughtful Sam Stoller.

Glickman sniffs the air. "Hey guys, forget about last night. I smell Gold!"

He and Stoller punched their fists high in victory before continuing with their workout run.

"He has the right attitude," Jesse commented. "But those Jews are also walkin' into a den of lions."

"Think they'll get thrown out next?"

"Well, if they do, they'll still have a future," assessed Jesse. "Glickman isn't just a track star but a football one at Syracuse. And Stoller's no slouch at Michigan. They'll have jobs when this is over. You and I'll be back picking cotton."

"Ah, correction, a tobacco 'harvester.' You're the cotton picker!"

"Damn right. At age seven, carrying those heavy cotton bales smashed me down some. That's why my legs are shorter than yours!"

Jesse stooped over, pretending to be carrying a heavy bale.

The two laughed heartedly, enjoying each other's company.

Their brisk run had them catching up to Glickman and Stoller to stride together.

At that moment, John still was not sure of his future. All he knew was that lots of people back in Connellsville were counting on him for something great to make them proud. As always, he would let his long running legs do his talking.

CHAPTER 24

Berlin, Germany, July 1936

Nazi stormtroopers were monitoring *Juden Verboten* (Jews forbade), and *Juden Unerwuenscht* (Jews not Wanted) boards and slogans became taken down at Berlin stores, hotels, and beer gardens as the Reich tried to hide their virulent racism from the tourists.

A stormtrooper gave an order to a hotel owner.

"Hide all Anti-Jew signs until the Olympics are over."

The hotel owner gave a Nazi salute in understanding.

When the soldier left, the Hotel Owner whispered to his wife. "How can they do this to their own people? I hope the world doesn't judge us."

His worried wife asked, "How far can Hitler take this?"

"There's no telling."

Swastika fans adorn Berlin for 1936 Olympics.

CHAPTER 25

Bremerton, Germany, July 1936

At the end of July 1936, the USS *Manhattan* cruise liner docked in Germany at Bremerton, close to Hamburg. After being greeted warmly by the German citizens, they took a train to Berlin. There, Long John and other American athletes got aboard a double-decker bus to follow a marching band up *Unter den Linden* to the City Halls steps, where the Mayor of Berlin awaited them.

Jesse Owens, John Woodruff, and members of the 1936 U.S. Olympic team arrive in Berlin, circa July 26. (National Archives, courtesy of USHMM Photo Archives.)

Germans greet the arrival of the U.S. Olympic team to the 1936 Olympics in Berlin. (National Archives, courtesy of USHMM Photo Archives.)

The scene was chaotic as Jesse Owens, Long John, and other black American athletes became mobbed by young Germans seeking photos and autographs.

A young German carrying a camera asked, "*Bitte, das foto?*"

Jesse was very accommodating. "Sure."

He and Woodruff allowed the crowds to snap photos and to touch them.

Young Woodruff became amazed. "They're fascinated by the color of our skin!"

Jesse showed the cuffs of his shirt, sticking out from his sports jacket. "Someone used scissors to snip off pieces of my clothing!"

Woodruff understood. "Souvenirs, Jess, souvenirs. They're treating us like royalty!"

"They look at blacks differently," Jesse guessed. "It's like we're not something they see in their daily life. We're not threatening to them."

"I think they admire us," Young Woodruff said. "I'll take it."

They suddenly became somber when viewing large banners hanging about of "Aryan" athletes in a heroic pose, blue-eyed blondes with powerful, finely chiseled features running and throwing.

"Are these guys our competition?" John asked Jesse.

"Who knows? We'll soon find out."

They soon were made aware that Germany skillfully promoted the Olympics with colorful posters and magazine spreads. Powerful imagery drew a link between Nazi Germany and ancient Greece, symbolizing the Nazi racial myth that a superior German civilization was the rightful heir of an "Aryan" culture of classical antiquity. This vision of classical antiquity emphasized the idea of "Aryan" racial types: heroic, blue-eyed blonds with finely chiseled features.

Inside a Berlin restaurant, John, Jesse, and other black athletes were sitting among whites at tables.

"The red carpets are rolled out for us," Woodruff said in amazement.

"Are these Krauts color blind?" Jesse asked.

Propaganda-posing photo of bare-chested German athletes in 1936 Berlin Olympics.

German 1936 Olympics "To the Glory" postcard.

Woodruff just shook his head. "No segregation, none at all. We can eat where we want and go into any places that whites do. No restrictions. This freedom is how it should be."

John then became transfixed by a sea of swastika-insignia black and red flags one hundred feet high lined up in long rows. It was an ominous sight, like some tidal waves about to crash down upon those who got in its way. Stormtroopers were just about everywhere.

"Never seen anything so intimidating," he said to his group.

White athletes Glickman and Stollar sat at a table alongside them, with Glickman asking, "Know what the swastika symbol stands for?"

"Ah, not really," Woodruff said honestly.

Glickman used a mock-scholarly voice: "It was an ancient religious Icon in the culture of Eurasia, used as a symbol of divinity and spirituality in Indian religion. The Nazis, unfortunately, transformed the meaning into anti-Semitism and terror."

Glickman and Stoller knew much about Jewish and German relations. They and many others believed Hitler thought the German (Aryan race) was superior to all others.

"Hitler is obsessed with 'racial purity,'" Glickman went on. "He truly feels his idea of a 'pure' German race has to control the world. And he believes that Aryan superiority is being threatened, particularly by the Jews."

"Scary stuff," Jesse tossed into the traffic pattern of conversation.

Stoller felt the same. "Best, we watch each other's backs."

Jesse nodded to Long John

"Count us in," Woodruff said.

CHAPTER 26

Berlin, July 1936 – Olympic Village, "The Village of Peace"

The Village housing all the competing athletes from various countries around the world was elaborate, like a college campus. The 130-acre village, constructed by the German army under the direction of Captain Wolfgang Fuerstner, lay in the middle of a magnificent forest of birch. Beautiful lawns rolled down to an artificial lake and a small cluster of blue ponds. The primary sector of the Olympic village was in the shape of a downward pointing horseshoe. Close to the apex of the horseshoe design was the main hall and general service building. A smaller annex was located above the top of the horseshoe, and a second smaller village was situated to the bottom.

John Woodruff was excited to be at his first Olympics and visiting Berlin. He walked the city's beautiful boulevards going through its center to Brandenburg Gate. Along the way, he saw movie houses catering to worldwide tastes. The new craze was *Mickey Mouse,* and films with American actresses Greta Garbo and Jean Harlow were big hits. Woodruff would also never forget the tourists and visitors coming to applaud the finest athletes in the world.

Woodruff and roommate Mack Robinson, the older brother of famed baseball great Jackie Robinson, strolled through the village, seeing a couple of American athletes with young women and babies; several team members had brought wives and other relatives along with them.

Young John Woodruff and the other athletes were in awe over the Olympic Village's movie theater, small shopping area, a well-staffed and

Mack Robinson, 200-meter Silver Medal '36 Olympic runner, brother of
baseball great Jackie Robinson, and Woodruff's roommate at Olympic Village.

stocked hospital specializing in sports medicine, postal facilities, recreational swimming, exercise areas, backwoods walking trails, and plenty of dining facilities. Training facilities in the Village included a four-hundred-meter oval track and a full-size indoor swimming pool. Animals such as squirrels scampered around. Swans, imported into the village, enhanced the ambiance. Mosquito breeding grounds were destroyed.

The athletes would be lodging in huts. There were two stewards always on duty in each house who spoke the athletes' native language.

Inside the cafeteria was another site to behold. The Norddeutscher Lloyd shipping line provided catering: they probably had the best experience in Germany in catering to a large number of foreign clientele on their ships.

For each visiting team, the caterers prepared at the *Restaurant of the Nations* a comprehensive list of their gastronomic likes and dislikes. Specialty food items were imported in large quantities so that every reasonable wish of every athlete could be accommodated. The diner facilities could accommodate twenty-four thousand guests.

The record books tell how in three weeks the participants consumed 100 cows, 91 pigs, over 650 lambs, 8,000 pounds of coffee, 150,000 pounds of vegetables, and 160,000 pints of milk.

Fuhrer Hitler was a teetotaler and the order for the athletes was no drinking. However, the French and Italians railed against the idea of no wine, while the Belgians and Dutch thought the prospect of no beer was too much to contemplate. All four nations were the exceptions and were served alcohol at every meal after they protested.

Long John Woodruff was quite happy to see that they had plenty of spaghetti, his favorite, in the Olympic Village. Captain Wolfgang Fuerstner who constructed the Olympic Village often checked in on the athletes. He heard of Woodruff's concern for spaghetti, something Long John hoped they had, and Fuerstner made sure John was offered ample kinds.

To which Woodruff gave him repeated waves to say thank you.

Two German athletes befriended John and roommate Robinson.

"Your English is pretty good," assessed Woodruff.

"Yours too."

They shared a laugh, and then John asked, "What do you feel about Hitler?"

The young German answered, "He's done a lot for the country, economically speaking."

However, the other German countered, "Yeah, but he's despicable in other ways!"

He gestured to a wall behind them to the athletes' entertainment center building with a giant bas-relief of menacing, marching German soldiers carrying rifles in front.

"The Olympic Village is called the 'Village of Peace.' Marching German soldiers with rifles are hardly peaceful."

"True," was all John said.

The German athlete, wary of Hitler, added, "Maybe it gives a hint of Hitler's military ambitions."

Stormtroopers walking about looked toward the athletes. The two German athletes quickly walked away from the Americans, not wanting to draw suspicion by talking to them.

Mack Robinson assessed the situation. "I guess no matter where you go, things are screwed up. People aren't content."

Woodruff, Robinson, and the other American athletes were feeling a niggling doubt that all was not well in Germany.

Meanwhile, in Berlin, the festivities went on, and everyone ignored the danger as the world stood poised on the verge of war. Yet for fifteen glorious days in August of 1936, joy, excitement, and friendly competition made the world forget.

Long John in Berlin posing with two other international athletes and a German Soldier. (Courtesy of University of Pittsburgh.)

CHAPTER 27

Reichssportfiled Olympic Stadium, 1936

Woodruff and his American teammates eventually found their way into the vast expanse of Berlin Stadium. For John, comparing it to Fayette Field in Connellsville was like seeing a hummingbird next to an ostrich.

Hitler had demanded that the new Olympic Stadium be the biggest in the world, outstripping the previous most enormous Olympic Stadium in Los Angeles built for their 1932 Games. The Berlin Stadium had seats for one-hundred thousand spectators but could hold one-hundred and ten thousand. The stadium was white, towering high and long; it did not remind one of a building as much as some Titanic-sized battleship. In addition to the stadium, was a swimming facility, hockey rink, theater, sports field, and many outbuildings and parking areas. In all, 150 other new Olympic buildings became completed in time for the event.

Long John said in awe to Jesse, "The size of this place! Bigger than my hometown!"

"The largest arena in the world," Jesse exclaimed.

As the international athletes went through practice routines, the Americans noted the continued fascination coaches and scientists had with the American blacks. John Woodruff's long strides and the graceful legs of Jesse Owens became obsessively scrutinized. Larry Snyder, Owens' outspoken forty-year-old Ohio State coach, and another coach observed the Germans studying Owens.

"Just look at those coaches studying Jess like he's a rare specimen of fauna!"

Dean Cromwell, the bow-tied US sprint coach, got in on the conversation. He was with Larson Robertson, the US head coach. The fifty-year-old, with a limp, walked with a cane.

"Well, their sprinting and jumping brings them close to their primitive world," Cromwell said in a bigoted style.

Snyder did not let the comment slide. "Are you serious with that kind of racial crap?"

Cromwell nodded and continued, "Negroes are built for that. It was a life-and-death matter in the jungle."

Snyder mumbled to himself, "Jesus! What a bigot!"

Robertson shook his head and went back to observing his athletes, while Snyder walked away in disgust. He saw some American black athletes called into the medical office clinic inside the stadium, his athlete Jesse Owens among them.

Snyder followed them inside to see the American black athletes becoming examined by white doctors scrutinizing their muscles and bones.

One doctor turned to another to say in German, "I believe they'll set world records. Notice the elongated heel bone; it's rare in the Caucasian race."

The second doctor agreed. "That long heel bone, the high arch, flat feet, longer tendons in the calf muscles, and long lower limbs are the keys to the Negroes' success in sprinting."

A third doctor gave his assessment. "We'll see if your conclusions are correct."

Snyder got in between the doctors and Jesse. "*Sprichst du Englisch?*"

The first doctor answered, "*Ja.* We speak English."

"Gentlemen," Snyder went on, "please do your calculations quickly. You're interrupting our athletes' training."

Another doctor took resentment. "Our medical conclusions are crucial to these examinations."

Snyder did not back down. "I don't give a damn about your medical conclusions. Go examine your German team!"

When he noticed a doctor with a needle getting close to Jesse, he got in the way. "*Whoa! Whoa!* No needles, no pills, no nothin' gets near these boys!"

Another German doctor did not like the interference of his American. "I don't recognize you being the coach of Owens?"

"At Ohio State University, I am!" Snyder spat. "Over here, I'm his agent, and also for some of the others." He winked to Woodruff. "Right, Long John?"

"Ah, that's right, agent Snyder," John answered.

A frequent poster displayed in Berlin during 1936 Olympic Games.

Snyder glanced at his watch. "Okay, docs, wrap it up. We're out of here."

Along the Berlin streets, radio towers and large television screens were everywhere.

A Tour Guide spoke to a group of visiting fans surrounding her.

"Over three-thousand radio programs will transmit these Olympics worldwide in various languages," she informed. "The Games will also be the first to be broadcast on television. Twenty-eight eight-by-ten-foot screen monitors are set up around the city, allowing locals and tourists to follow the Games free of charge. Furthermore, three cameras six-feet long each looking like cannons will be filming the athletes in action."

The Berlin streets were elaborate public spectacles laden with choreographed pageantry.

Woodruff was among a group of American black athletes who strolled about. They and writers and fans moving about the big city were witness to the mighty Nazi propaganda machine. These Olympics marked the most significant "sport and theater" spectacle to date; the writers wrote back to America. They rose to new heights of art to give new meaning to staging elaborate public displays and rallies, choreographed pageantry, and warm German hospitality.

No one hated these German citizens, for they knew they were getting caught up in Hitler's rousing exultation. Many felt he was the most powerful man on earth, bar none. Some black athletes with John were impressed by everything.

"Never have I seen anything like this in our country, man!" Ralph Metcalf exclaimed. "This is . . . huge!"

Mack Robinson, though, was suspicious. "These soldiers with rifles give me the creeps."

"Yeah," agreed Jesse Owens. "But the German people seem seduced, like on a drug or something."

The Berlin Stadium's vast expanse was incredible. Hitler had demanded that the new Olympic Stadium be the biggest in the world. In total, over 7.5 million tickets were sold for the events, this became viewed as a success, and most events saw full crowds.

On that clear-blue-sky opening day of the Olympics on August 1, 1936, Adolf Hitler, in the brown uniform of a Storm Trooper and wearing high leather boots, left the chancellery in an open touring car. At one point, he stood to give his standard salute, a limp over-the-shoulder flap.

Behind Hitler followed a long row of Mercedes convertibles that carried various dignitaries, politicians, and Olympic officials. The column moved slowly along the Via Triumphalis; forty thousand Nazi guardsmen were holding back the crowd lining the boulevard twenty to thirty people deep.

The crowd was yelling, "*Heil Hitler, Sieg Heil! Sieg Heil!*" and proudly holding their hands in stiff-arm salute.

To the foreigners watching, it had a bone-chilling effect. They could see how Germans were all under Hitler's hypnotic spell. Though many outside of Germany were calling Hitler's *Mein Kampf* impenetrable nonsense, many Nazi Germans looked at it as a bible of sorts.

When the procession reached the stadium, Hitler, and two Olympic officials, strode forward. Fuhrer Hitler emerged into the stadium, facing the vast crowd of spectators as a fanfare of thirty trumpets announced his arrival.

The colossal bell echoed a reverberating boom that announced the start of the Parade of Nations. Shortly before the arrival of Adolf Hitler to declare the Games open, the vast airship *Hindenberg* crossed ominously low over the packed stadium while trailing the Olympic flag on a long weighted line suspended from its gondola.

Hitler made it to the field as a small blond girl, wearing a blue dress, bound by a chaplet of flowers, came forward and, making a pretty German curtsey, gave him a bouquet of roses.

The opening Games spectacle was a colorful event. Some details, however, were out of the ordinary. Passing below the Fuhrer's booth, the

Hitler at Opening of Olympic Games ceremony being handed flowers by a little girl.

Austrian team gave the Nazi salute: the crowd cheered loudly. To the surprise of almost everyone, the Bulgarians goose-stepped by him. The two-hundred-and fifty-member French team received the most consider-able applause, whose salute was more Roman than Olympian, which they would later say was the case. The British did not lift their eyes to the Fuhrer and got booed.

Later in the alphabetical list of the foreign teams is the *Vereinigten Staaten,* the United States. On passing below Hitler's booth, all the pre-vious groups had lowered their national flags. As expected, Woodruff and the other Americans—in with their white trousers, blue jackets, and straw hats with the red, white, and blue band—refused to honor Hitler and kept their flags raised.

It became apparent that Hitler's searing blue eyes did not like what they were seeing, but he held his composure. He did not have the time to put on one of his rages. Just as the dipped American passed beneath his reviewing stand, the German team striding eight abreast emerged from the Marathon Gate.

In all-white uniforms and yachting caps—perhaps in tribute to the yacht-loving Kaiser Wilhelm II—they marched onto the track, the musi-cians under Richard Strauss' baton again performing "*Deutschland*" and the "*Horst Wessel*" song. As the German team reached a point on the track directly below Hitler's booth, the entire body of spectators raised from their stadium seats to give the "*Heil Hitler*" salute, and held it until the German team took its place at the far end of the field.

Writer Thomas Wolfe, who was there, described the opening as an "almost religious event, the crowd screaming, swaying in unison and begging for Hitler." There was something scary about it, his cult of personality.

Virtually everyone in the stadium knew that this was homage to Hitler, for, at this point, some were calling him the German Caesar. In addition to that Hitler was with his group watching the competition—the short, cadaverous thin scarecrow Goebbels; the sweating, massive and round-faced Herman Goering; and Heinrich Himmler, whose weak chin, diminutive physique, and round-black rimmed glasses make one forget that he is the absolute ruler of the SS, Gestapo and every other police force in the country.

Although no German or visitor now to Germany dare spoke aloud of it, the joke making the rounds among foreigners in Berlin about the three of them. Describe the ideal Aryan? Why, he is as blonde as Hitler, as slim as Goering and as tall as Goebbels! Hitler argued that the German (he wrongly described them as the Aryan race) was superior to all others. Hitler was obsessed with 'racial purity.' He used the word 'Aryan' to describe his idea of a 'pure German race' or Herrenvolk. The 'Aryan race' had a duty to control the world.

The Nazis believed that the Aryans had the most "pure blood" of all the people on earth. The ideal Aryan had pale skin, blond hair, and blue eyes. Non-Aryans became seen as impure and even evil. Hitler believed that Aryan superiority was being threatened, particularly by the Jews. A league table of 'races' was created with Aryans at the top and with Jews, Gypsies, and black people at the bottom. (He called the American black athletes at the Games "auxiliary athletes.") These 'inferior' people became seen as a threat to the purity and strength of the German nation.

CHAPTER 28

Reichssportfiled Olympic Stadium, 1936

The Berlin Olympiad opened as a salute to the new German monarch. On the fringes of the track, boys from the Hitler Youth opened their small wire cages. Twenty-five thousand white doves flew up into the sky. A distant battery of guns hammered out a twenty-one-gun salute.

U.S. distance runner Louis Zamperini was laughing as Woodruff observed him relating it to a newsman's camera.

"They released 25,000 pigeons, the sky was a cloud with pigeons, they circled overhead, and then they shot a cannon and they scared the poop out of the pigeons, as we had straw hats, flat straw hats, and you could hear the pitter-patter on our straw hats. But we felt sorry for the women, for they got it in their hair, but I mean there was a mass of droppings, and I say it was so funny . . ."

Hitler, now standing in his private seating box with his entourage, approached the microphone and, for once, he had no speech to make. He simply declared: "I announce the opening of the Games of Berlin, celebrating the Eleventh Olympiad in the modern era."

Shortly after that, when it became silent, a twenty-six-year-old runner, Siegfried Eifrig, appeared from the tunnel below. Handsome, he personified the Aryan race—tall, blond, blue-eyed, and athletic.

The runner held the torch above his head as he ran across the track and up the steps to a marble platform. And there he lifted himself on his toes and plunged the torch into a concrete bowl. Flames leaped from the cauldron.

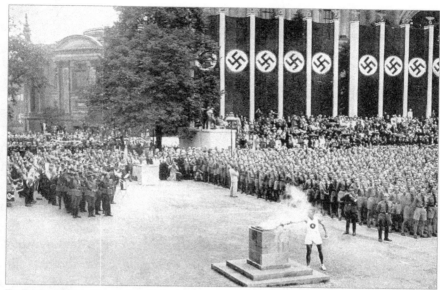

The Torch Lighting ceremony at Berlin Games.

Equally as impressive was that first torch's relay, which just ended in the new stadium. The torch was passed by no less than three-thousand and seventy-five torchbearers, each running slightly more than half a mile of the journey from Greece to the Berlin Olympic Stadium.

The 1936 Olympic Games were just the third Olympics to have an Olympic Torch. The Nazis wanted to make sure theirs was unique, so they chose to have a torch be lit in Greece, using the sun's rays, at the site of the first-ever Olympics. The torch would then travel across Europe until it reached Berlin, finally lighting the Olympic Cauldron. Today, the torch became transmitted across the world in this same format, and it became regarded as the start of the modern-day Olympic torch relay.

Among the many celebrities in attendance was trans-Atlantic aviator legend, Charles Lindbergh, a special guest of the Germans. In another section was world heavyweight champ, Max Schmeling, with his beautiful actress wife, Anny Ondra.

Schmeling was Germany's symbol of Aryan supremacy after he knocked out American rising star Joe Louis just months before these

Olympics. The Nazi's viewed him and their Party as invincible. However, Louis, in a rematch in 1938, knocked out Schmeling in the first round.

With so many other celebrities about Berlin Stadium, many spectators found themselves especially intrigued by one female in particular, and she was not a competing athlete. It was an athlete-turned-dancer-turned-filmmaker. The great Leni Riefenstahl, whom several film historians were soon-to-be calling the most celebrated documentary filmmaker ever. Leni was strikingly beautiful in her own right, and her acting in the film *The White Hell of Piz Palu* brought her into the limelight in Germany and beyond.

Riefenstahl began setting up very odd but creative camera angles never seen before to film the Olympics. Even in the sky above the stadium, she had cameras in a vast massive airship to capture the Olympics. Leni was making the 1936 Olympic film called *Olympia,* the first film ever made on the Olympics. This film that glorified the Olympics would go down in history as a dazzling, visual poem or meditation on muscle and movement at the Games. *Time Magazine* would later call this two-part film released in 1938 as one of all-time greatest 100 films. The shots Riefenstahl directed, overseeing eighty of Germany's finest cameramen, would be haunting, almost hypnotic. She pioneered new artistry in the filming of sporting events, installing numerous strategic positions, and accumulating their material for a celluloid record of the stirring events.

The athletes could not help but notice her, with Glickman leading the way.

"Leni Riefenstahl—Hitler's favorite film director. *Va-va voom!* What a knockout!"

Long John also commented. "She uses a camera like it's a microscope."

To which Glickman replied, "That lovely *fraulein* can inspect me as close as she wants!"

"Ah," one of the athletes began when seeing Leni going to film American decathlon great, the handsome Glen Morris, "the rumor is that Riefenstahl and Morris have become more than friends."

Actress/filmmaker Leni didn't deny being close with Morris. She would belatedly write in her memoirs in 1987 that the affair had developed in Berlin while filming Olympia, the Berlin Olympic film. She also wrote of being in love with Morris, that he broke her heart. After the '36 Olympics, Hollywood called for Morris, and he starred in one film *Tarzan's Revenge* in 1938. He died at age 61.

Riefenstahl died at age 101.

CHAPTER 29

Reichssportfiled Olympic Stadium, 1936

The competition finally commenced with the shot-put event. Germany had never won an Olympic gold medal before, but, by three o'clock in the afternoon, they had triumphed in the first two events of the Berlin Games.

Hitler leaped to his feet, laughing and clapping. He could not have been more pleased by the outcome.

Winning the gold medal was Hans Woellke, a German policeman. Tilly Fleischer also set a new record in the women's javelin. Hitler soon invited both victors to his box—where he congratulated them in ostentatious style. He did the same with Ilmari Salminen, a tall blond Finn, who won the 10,000-meter final ahead of two of his countrymen. Hitler presided at the medal ceremonies and shook the winners' hands.

"That year, it became increasingly clear that Germany only wanted to see its superheroes in one light: the stars of the Aryan race, superior for their genetic makeup rather than their athleticism," said Barbara Burstin, a history lecturer at the University of Pittsburgh and Carnegie Mellon University. "It provided Hitler with a showcase. It was a propaganda bonanza for him."

But things were much different later that day when the high jump competition began. Black American athlete Cornelius Johnson won the gold medal with an Olympic-record leap of 6 feet, 8 inches. The silver

Hindenburg airship flying low over Berlin Stadium, opening day of the Games.

went to fellow black teammate David Albritton, at 6–6¾. The best German jumper, Gustav Weinkoetz, finished in a four-way tie for sixth.

Hitler did not like what he was witnessing. However, throughout the opening day and all of the fourteen days of athletic competition, he maintained a deliberately low-key presence at the Olympics. The dictator became one to please Olympic officials who did not want him to upstage the festivities. It was also an excellent opportunity for the *Führer*

Hitler giving the Nazi salute after first German Gold Medal win.

to appear calm and dignified among the thousands of international observers who were watching his every move.

Hitler had cautiously pale blue eyes beneath drooping lids—eyes that, for some reason, gave the impression that the man is considering a dozen things at once. Many throughout Germany and beyond knew that Hitler was some unearthly creation in the world. Mesmerizing, brilliant with words, but also given to fits of extreme rage. However, it became apparent that he was playing the role of the kind Fuhrer while the whole world watched him, even though he disliked the American blacks taking over the track proceedings.

Eventually, he signaled to his group that he wanted to see no more of this for today. His entourage left the stadium, as everyone who was near Hitler extended their hands in their usual stiff-armed salute.

John Woodruff, with Glickman and Stoller, observed the dictator leaving.

The humorous Glickman put his finger under his nose to mimic having a mustache as he wiggled around *a la Charlie Chaplin,* to the delight of Long John and Stoller.

"Who does Hitler remind you of?"

"My favorite film character, except he's real life."

Glickman held up a warning finger to the departing Hitler. "I can't wait to run that little prick out of the stadium!"

"The 800 gives me the first shot," Woodruff brought up. "I'll do my best to bring home the gold."

CHAPTER 30

Bungalow at Olympic Village, 1936

Track and Field head coach Lawson Robertson and running Coach Cromwell were having a private meeting with their seven relay runners, among them Glickman and Stoller. The two Jewish athletes wore shocked expressions during a heated talk with Cromwell.

"We can't take chances," Cromwell insisted. "Just heard that a supposedly "crack German squad" has been training in secret. Owens and Metcalf will replace Glickman and Stoller."

Glickman became livid. "This is ridiculous! How can you hide world-class sprinters?"

Jesse Owens intervened. "Coach, Glickman, and Stoller deserve to run. They qualified! This race is their big chance."

Cromwell pointed a finger into Jesse's chest. "You'll do as you're told!"

Glickman was desperate to run. "Coach, any combination of the seven teammates can win the race by fifteen yards. And I can't stress enough the significance of running and winning, as Jews, in front of Hitler."

Cromwell sighed. "I understand what you feel, but I'm entering my four best sprinters in the relay. In my judgment, Owens and Metcalfe are better than Stoller and you."

Glickman remained outspoken. "You know that Sam and I are the only two Jews on the track team."

"If we don't run," Stoller interjected, "there's bound to be a lot of criticism back home."

"We'll take our chances," Cromwell answered steadfastly.

A sulking Glickman sat on the bench.

Glickman and Stoller became the next victims. There had always been a purity of track and field. Those who ran the fastest, jumped the highest, and threw farthest made the team. Very cut and dry. Cromwell and Brundage changed all that.

Glickman had suspicions about the fairness of the relay team selection process that began at the American Olympic team trials in New York when announced he placed fifth of the seven runners competing in the sprint finals.

They did not have finish line photography at the races as in modern times, yet films of the race indicated that Glickman finished third behind Owens and Metcalf.

The Glickman controversy was something John knew well. However, the judges, apparently under pressure from Cromwell, placed Glickman fifth behind Draper and Wycoff. As a result, Glickman was not one of the three sprinters entered in the 100-yard dash, a premier Olympic event. Instead, Glickman and Stoller traveled to Berlin as part of the 400-yard relay team, each scheduled to run a 100-yard leg of the race.

Outside in the Olympic Village, young Long John went to the sad two Jewish runners. "I heard what happened. It's not fair."

Glickman kicked at the ground. "Cromwell is kowtowing to the Nazis by removing Stoller and me."

"Why's he doing it?" Woodruff asked.

"To spare Hitler the embarrassment of two Jews on the victory podium," Glickman assured.

Stoller became deflated. "This is so humiliating."

Glickman put a consoling arm around his crestfallen friend.

CHAPTER 31

The Most Daring Move Ever in Track, August 4, 1936

The first-round of Olympic heats for the 800-meter run was on August 2nd, and Woodruff's running made a lifeless impression. The towering lad finally managed to secure a third-place (in 1:58.7) to be able to advance.

"'I've got a cold, my chest is hurting,' was my excuse for not do-ing better," Old John recalled. "Following my mom's recipe, I consumed large quantities of honey to recover instead of the tonics that the coaches recommended."

In the semis that took place the next day, Woodruff seemed to be back on form, winning his in 1:52.7—the fastest heat of all three—and quickly taking the measure of the Polish hope, Kucharski. After that, there was the golden end-race taking place on August 4. In almost all those races, he became seriously pocketed in the middle of the pack. In the 800-meter semi-finals, John ran away from the field, winning 20 yards over Kazamiere of Poland and Carlos Anderson of Argentina, in that order.

Arthur Daley of the New York Times, who wrote then "if the other half-milers are smart enough to keep cutting in front of Woodruff and force him to chop that gigantic stride of his, they may beat him. But if they let him get out by himself, he should breeze in!"

How prophetically right Daley proved to be.

August 4th – The Race for the Gold

Hitler, again in his gleaming entourage of Mercedes convertibles, swept through the Nazi-controlled city on its way to Berlin Stadium. The day was gray and overcast.

The massive stadium, with one-hundred and ten-thousand spectators, was surrounded by black and red swastikas fluttering against a leaden sky. Thirty trumpets sounded to announce Hitler's arrival into the stadium, as brown-shirted Stormtroopers stood shoulder to shoulder like an iron fence.

Hitler moved to his private box, followed by several high-ranking officers: Goebbels, Goering, and Himmler. The shriek from 110,000 throats of fans was deafening, "Heil Hitler! Sieg Heil! Sieg Heil!"

The dictator returned their proud outstretched arm salute with one of his own before he and his entourage sat as binoculars were handed to him. Focusing binoculars to the athletic field below, the German dictator studied the lineup of runners only to settle his concentration on the lone American—a long ebony-skinned Negro.

Hitler asked Goebbels, "Is this the giant Negro who ran in the preliminaries?"

"Yes. Der Neger's name is Woodruff. They call him Long John."

Hitler's group continued to monitor from their towering height the young John Woodruff wearing number 745—a gangly young kid from the coal and coke mines of western Pennsylvania.

Woodruff appeared focused beyond belief. Hitler, Stormtroopers, Swastika flags, and Aryan supremacy meant nothing to him. He settled into his crouched position at the starting line. The cleats on the balls of his shoes dug holes in the cinders from which to thrust.

John lined up with Phil Edwards of Canada; Italy's Mario Lanzi, Anderson, Williamson, Hornbostel, and Kucharsky; McCabe of England; and Backhouse of Australia.

Everything happened so fast in Berlin. John was not a household name and in the spotlight like Jesse Owens. He and his teammates saw

Hitler coming into the stadium with his entourage and the stormtroopers. Those soldiers stood shoulder to shoulder like an iron fence. Then came the roar of '*Heil,* Hitler!' from 110,000 troops, spectators' arms outstretched. That got his attention.

However, young Woodruff quickly forgot everything at the starting line. His deep concentration focused on nothing but winning. The other athletes in the event were sizing up Woodruff, wondering how to offset his enormous stride.

At the starting line, limbering up oblivious to everything in the background, Long John concentrated on the task at hand. With the sheen of sweat on him, he indeed was a full-fledged Olympian athlete of high gloss. He whispered to himself, "This is the moment, *my* moment. Hear nothing but that big mean locomotive breathing down your back."

As he got into his final crouching stance, he again whispered, "Mom and Dad, this is for you."

So intensely concentrating, John was oblivious to Director Leni Riefenstahl and crew close by in position, nor she and her crew's close-up filming of athletes and spectators in the crowd, achieved with a 600 Leica lens.

John wondered long after that day why he chose the strategy in the finals not to take the lead in this race as he usually did in his races and even in the Berlin preliminaries. His coaches did not give him much advice on how to run. They knew what John could do, so he was expected just to go out and do it. He did not even consult his coaches in Berlin.

Woodruff got in position, crouching as the balls of his feet dug holes in the cinders from which to thrust out.

The German starter, a bulky, balding German, said: "*auf die platz . . . Fertig!*" just before the gun cracked loud and flat in the immense silence. But it was a false start, and the race had to begin over. This time the gun cracked, sending Long John Woodruff into track history.

Amidst all the cheering and screaming from the 10,000-plus spectators, Woodruff heard little of it. As he said, "You see, when you're running a race, you're concentrating on what you're doing. You may hear the noise, but you can't hear anything distinctly."

Woodruff did remember the *absence* of one sound during the early going of the 800-meter final—that of labored breathing.

Phil Edwards, a black man from Canada, set the pace. He had run in two previous Olympics. John was using a strategy of running in the second position, laying back and waiting. But the pace of Edwards was slow for the first 400 meters. It was only fifty-seven seconds, and at that time, John ran at least fifty-one seconds. The duo was followed closely by Anderson, Williamson, and Hornbostel.

As they went to the second lap backstretch, John took the lead, but only for an instant, as Edwards moved around him.

Edwards set a slow pace for the race, one that had John's long stride wasted as he was a young, novice runner against these experienced veteran runners. Soon, he found himself boxed in. John was unable to break through the pack because he was afraid he might foul somebody, get spiked, or be disqualified.

"So, what to do?" he asked himself. He was frustrated and disgusted, so he stopped. With three-hundred and fifty meters left to the race, he stopped and let all the runners precede him. It appeared to everyone that he had either given up or just had lost the race.

Slowing, stopping for a brief moment and dead last, Long John began taking off again, his head held back high as he reared forward. On the outside lane, long legs loping and running extra meters, but John poured it on at the home stretch like a smoky freight train! He could hear his heartbeats *thump, thump, thump,* and heavy even breathing—a well-oiled machine straining to its limits.

He ran all around them and won the race, even though he had the handicap.

Waves of sweat drizzled off Long John's powerful body as he snapped his limbs back and forth like a lethal machine. He refused anyone stopping him from reaching his goal. Woodruff's long, powerful stride passed the leaders, and his miraculous come-from-behind victory brought thousands in Berlin Stadium to their feet and thrilled the hearts of Americans tuned to the radio that supplied the details of the run.

Long John opening up his immense stride, heading to the front of the 800-meter finals race (German souvenir Olympic postcard which reads on the back: "With improbably long steps the Negro Woodruff ran toward the goal of the 800m to win.")

A sportswriter from the *New York Herald-Tribune*, Jesse Abramson, who was covering the Games wrote, that what John did was "the most daring move ever seen on a track."

He stopped and lagged back to the last place. While everyone passed, he got spiked by another runner who was not expecting the sudden movement. He did not even realize it until he saw the blood on his leg after the race.

Woodruff's move was all the more audacious because of a fundamental rule of running: any time a movement was out of the ordinary, it created more force against you, so it slowed you down. Not only was the foot placement thrown off but also the arm movement.

Sportswriters wrote that he was an excellent strategist able to determine the pace of a race quickly, and then shift into gear, which is what he had to do to win the 800 in Berlin. By stopping, he was able to rid himself of the other seven runners, and then he went after them. They never dreamed that he was going to pass them after having to stop, but they were in for the surprise of their lives. No one in the world could

Woodruff crossing the finish line first in 800-meter run to win Gold.
(Courtesy of University of Pittsburgh.)

have run that race that way. Some even described it as briefly walking to win the running race!

He moved out into the third lane, stepped on the gas, and let his long stride make up for the lost time. It was not an easy race after that. He would swap the lead twice with Edwards down the homestretch. He began charging for the finish line in his long, lengthening stride until, with one final burst of speed, he took the lead and held it to the tape in 1:52.9, beating out Lanzi.

The Italian, so frustrated by not being able to catch Woodruff, punched his fist at the air in total frustration.

Winning that race had him becoming the first American black runner to win Gold at Berlin. It also marked the first time in twenty-four years that the United States had won an 800 Gold Medal. The last American to win before that was Ted Meredith in 1912, with the British runners dominating the meet in between.

Woodruff's opponents were all smart, experienced runners, so he had to win the medal the hard way, on ability and courage against all the odds. Snell thought had he not been boxed and forced to go outside if he could have led all the way; then, he may have set a world record.

Not only had Leni Riefenstahl captured the event on film but also the award-winning American filmmaker and director Bud Greenspan.

After the race, Long John quietly walked off the track.

There was no celebrating on the track after the race as they do in modern times. He merely went to his black runner teammates and said rousingly, "I just punched the first hole into Hitler's Master Race Theory. Now go and punch some more. Whoop 'em good!"

The runners became intoxicated by John's win.

White teammates also came to congratulate Woodruff, led by the glib Glickman, who quipped, "I just bet on you to win the Kentucky Derby! That was amazing, simply amazing!"

"Thanks, Marty."

However, his coaches said nothing to him. Nothing.

At the race's finish, the enormous Olympic scoreboard posted the winner: *Woodruff, USA*

American flags throughout the inside of the stadium began to rise—thousands of small ones held by spectators throughout the stands. The victory had added significance for Woodruff, ending the belief that the Americans could not win that particular event.

John Woodruff, the world's newest running star, mounted the victor's platform. An olive wreath—representing victory—was placed on his head by a beautiful blond German girl. It was the last time the olive wreaths were used in the Olympics until the 2004 Athens Games. The medals were not on the ribbons like they are today, where they put them around one's neck. Woodruff's medal was in a little case, and they just handed it to him.

When John was up on the stand, they were playing *The Star-Spangled Banner* for all the Americans. Woodruff recalled, "Then they had young girls coming over and presenting the medal. It kind of did something to a person."

Woodruff on Berlin podium accepting Gold Medal while holding Olympic Tree sapling. (Courtesy of University of Pittsburgh.)

Goebbels was also there, and as he limped toward the victor's stand, Woodruff lowered his head so the German Propaganda Minister could hand the American his gold medal.

John was a bit confused, for none of the American athletes had practiced as to how they were supposed to respond. He was not quite sure whether to give the Nazi salute or the American salute. Woodruff went through three or four gyrations of how to salute until his heart told him what to do. Putting his hand on his heart, he saluted Hitler in the American manner as the Star-Spangled Banner played on.

John kept an eye on Hitler as well as Goebbels. He knew that they did not think much of blacks, and Goebbels would later talk in private, saying that the victories by them were a "disgrace."

Goebbels forced himself to use his best demeanor when presenting Woodruff his medal. His prowess went far beyond his physical limitations. Goebbels was highly educated with a Ph.D. in German literature

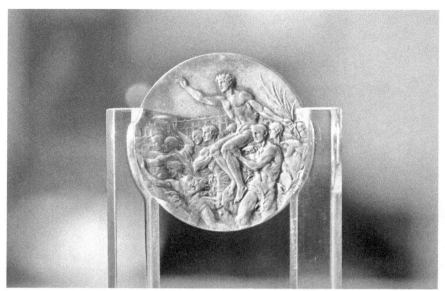

John Woodruff 800-meter Berlin Gold Medal. (Courtesy of University of Pittsburgh.)

and employed propaganda methods ahead of his time to enable Hitler and his Nazi party to secure their way to absolute power.

Hitler, wearing a revolting expression, left his box seat.

The Fuhrer hated seeing a black athlete, victorious. And surely Goebbels would have preferred to pin that medal on a cow. Regardless, for the black athletes, it was a very proud moment.

Goebbels left the podium area to confront filmmaker Leni Riefenstahl who had just filmed John's electrifying race, advising her: "Just concentrate on the Nazi cause and forget the rest."

"I will not!"

"I insist your cameras switch off when der negers are beating our athletes."

The director stood her ground. "I'm filming the Olympics for the—"

"—The Nazi Party!"

"No, the International Olympic Committee!" Leni shot back. "If you don't like it, then get your own cameras! Just keep away from mine!"

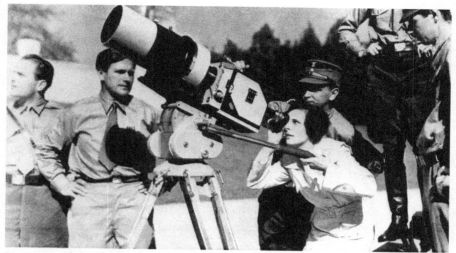

Filmmaker Leni Riefenstahl continuing to film for the International Olympic Committee, not the Nazi cause.

Goebbels forced himself to keep his composure. To a subordinate, he whispered, "Make this wild woman's life miserable!"

Jesse Owens also had a significant hand in crushing Hitler's myth of Aryan supremacy. He had given four virtuoso performances, winning Gold Medals in the 100-meter and 200-meter dashes, the long jump (called back then the broad jump), and next up for Owens was the 4 x 100-meter race.

Once again, the sprinters held a meeting on the field before the race. The coaches were there—Cromwell and Robertson.

Jesse again spoke his mind. "With their times, Glickman and Stoller deserve to run. Let them. I won three golds. I'm tired, beat. I've had enough."

Cromwell again pointed the finger at Jesse, "I told you before: do as you're told! Run!"

He stormed off.

Glickman and Stoller walked off dejectedly, heartbroken.

Watching the race from the bench, Glickman became overcome with mixed emotions as the US runners took off at a blistering speed, breaking the world record of the 400-meter relay in 39.8 seconds.

Shortly after that, Glickman observed America's four relay runners on the victory stand.

John Woodruff moved to Glickman and sat with him.

When Jesse Owens came off the victory stand, he went to Marty in a brave move. "That gold was yours, Marty. We all know that."

Glickman shook Jesse's hand. "If anything, I'm glad you won it. But we all know Brundage made the call for me not to run. He's an American Nazi and wanted to spare Hitler and his entourage the humiliation of seeing Jews on the podium!"

Hitler, under the tremendous roar of the crowd for America's relay team's victory, again left his box masking his disgust.

Hitler never stayed to watch a single black athlete receive the gold medal.

A German officer caught up to Hitler. "*Mein* Fuhrer, some of the chancelleries suggests it good propaganda to congratulate Jesse Owens on his record fourth Gold Medal."

"*Nein!*" Hitler grumbled. "Americans should be ashamed of letting *negers* win medals for them!"

"Yes, *Mein* Fuhrer, but perhaps . . ."

"*Nein!* I'll not allow a photograph of me shaking hands with a *neger!*"

The dictator left the stadium.

On Saturday, August 8, with Owens running the first leg of the relay race, the USA equaled the world record in the morning heat. Late that afternoon, in the final, Owens opened up a lead that Metcalf stretched even farther. Legendary *Daily News* sportswriter Gallo suggested that "they put the team so far out in front that the white boys to whom they turned over the baton could have crawled in on their hands and knees."

Hitler helped Owens win one of his medals since the Nazis demanded that one of the American runners in a relay race be replaced for being a Jew. Owens took that man's place and helped win the gold for the Americans.

Most people believed that Hitler snubbed all of the black athletes exclusively. Still, it was not because Hitler did not congratulate anybody that day except for the initial German winners, including his shot putter, Hans Woellke. But that had gotten him in trouble with the members of the Olympics committee. They told him that to maintain Olympic neutrality, and he would have to congratulate everyone or no one. Hitler chose to honor no one.

The crowd cheered wildly over Jesse Owens running the way he did. Owens had indeed prepared himself for a possible hostile reception. A coach had warned him not to be upset by anything that might happen in the stands. "Ignore the insults," Owens was told, "and you'll be all right."

Jesse winning four gold medals had gotten the most exceptional reception of his career at Berlin and satisfied blacks because it spoiled Hitler's planned victory party.

While 4,000 athletes from 49 different countries took part in 129 competitions, German Minister of Propaganda Joseph Goebbels wrote in his diary: *"After the Olympics, we'll get ruthless . . . Then there will be some shooting."*

But until then, youths like the twenty-one-year-old Woodruff were on top of the world. But there were other Olympians younger than him who were also in the limelight during those sixteen days in August, such as thirteen-year-old American diver Majorie Gestring who won the gold, making her the youngest ever to win gold at that time.

Connellsville, 2001

Under the Connellsville Woodruff Tree, Old John kept on reminiscing. "I suppose we all have an extraordinary moment in life, that fifteen minutes of fame or whatever they call it. Mine was for exactly one minute and fifty-two seconds."

The attentive teen listener asked, "What did it feel like?"

"Magical . . . like I was alone in the stadium. I couldn't even hear the roar of the audience, but I knew I'd done something exceptional. As I've said, my objective any time I got into a race was to win. I never thought in terms of taking second or third, I only thought in terms of winning. And that's what I did, in that big Olympic race and all the races that I ran. Determination. That's what it takes. I was winning for me, and I was winning for the country. Me first, then the country. It was definitely a special feeling to win the Gold Medal as a man of color. We destroyed Hitler's Master Race theory whenever we started winning those gold medals. I was very proud of that achievement, and I was delighted for myself and my country. Being the first African-American runner to win a gold medal, I know it motivated my black teammates to do the same."

The girl was in awe. "I'd give anything to have a magical moment like that."

"You will someday," John assured. "Just make sure you don't let it pass by."

"How will I know?"

"You just know, you'll feel it. The *New York Herald Tribune* called my stop-and-restart an unorthodox strategy 'the most daring move ever seen on a track.'"

"I'd say so."

CHAPTER 32

German Chancellery Building, 1936

A furious Hitler stomped before his chief advisors: the little scare-crow Goebbels and the sweating, massive, and round-faced Herman Goering—the second most powerful man in Germany.

The two men shared uncomfortable glances.

"Foreigners are turning our Nazi Olympics into a joke!" blurted the incensed Fuhrer. "I won't stand for it!"

Hitler lifted off the easel sheet showing the Olympic symbol banner of the two Aryan athletes in heroic poses, blonde and blue eyes, with powerful finely chiseled features, running and throwing. Large print at the bottom of the banner read: *Describe the ideal Aryan? Why, he's as blonde as Hitler, as slim as Goering, and as tall as Goebbels!*

Hitler's advisors squirmed even more when their leader ripped away from the banner displaying another one underneath.

"And this!"

The next banner shows two blond athletes painted black-skinned; their blond hair shaded in curly brown!

"Whoever slandered us will pay!"

Goebbels tried to appease the raging Fuhrer. "*Mein* Hitler, the Olympics will be over in days. Germany is still winning the medal count—"

"—Can't you see, you fools?" Hitler shouted in askance. "These American *negers* are turning our Master Plan into a joke!"

The listeners were at a loss for words.

CHAPTER 33

Connellsville, 2001

The elderly Woodruff continued to reminisce. "American Jewish athletes had it tough in Berlin, but so did the German Jews. It made these Nazi Olympics the "Games of Shame."

Old John closed his eyes and recalled.

Berlin Olympics, 1936

US athletes, including John and Glickman, strolled about the field watching athletic events. They reached the women's high jump competition and stopped to observe. Silence prevailed as an athlete concentrated before she attempted to clear the bar.

A tall young woman in her mid-twenties was standing by the competition. She knelt, a knee to the ground.

Glickman realized that she was stifling crying while clutching onto a tear-stained letter.

He moved to her to whisper, "You okay, miss?"

"I should be, since I'm about to win the bronze medal," the young female athlete answered in good English. "But I'm not."

"I don't understand," Glickman said.

"I'm Elfride Kaun, a German high jumper."

"Marty Glickman, American sprinter."

"My friend, Gretel Bergmann, should be here competing," Elfriede lamented. "We are the two best women jumpers in Germany."

"Why isn't she here?"

"Germany doesn't want her to compete because she's Jewish."

"Me too. I also wasn't allowed to run for America even though I qualified."

"Sorry to hear that," Elfriede said. "Gretel just sent me this telegram today, wishing me good luck. She also told what the German government wrote to her."

"May I ask what it says?"

"The German Olympic committee wrote to Gretel: 'Looking back on your recent performances, you could not possibly have expected to be chosen for the team . . .' It was signed '*Heil* Hitler.'"

Glickman listened to more before he said goodbye to Elfriede, and went back to his American teammates. He told them who Elfriede was and what the Germans did to Gretel Bergmann.

"And as a consolation for kicking Gretel Bergmann off the team, the Nazi authorities can offer you standing-room-only tickets for the women's track and field events, though expenses for transportation and hotel accommodations, unfortunately, cannot be supplied. Heil Hitler! The real reason she didn't compete was that Hitler didn't want a Jew competing for Germany. So hurt is Gretel that she didn't even answer Hitler's letter."

"As I said before," Glickman added, "We Jews and blacks are getting screwed every which way."

Glickman's word became quite true when he, Woodruff, and others in their group saw American black runner Louise Stokes on the sidelines crying as her race was running without her in the lineup. Stokes was predicted to be the first black American female to win Olympic gold. She was suddenly replaced by a white runner. As par for the course, no reason became given.

Still, German fans were getting autographs of American Black athletes, among them Long John Woodruff, who said to his black teammates, "Regardless of what Hitler thinks of us, the German fans surely love us!"

119

CHAPTER 34

Connellsville, Penna. – under the Woodruff Tree, 2001

Aged John continued recounting events of Gretel Bergmann. "I later found out that Gretel left Germany before the Olympics due to Jewish repression. She went instead to compete in England, but the German government forced her to return to high jump in the Olympics for her home country. Her family members who'd stayed in Germany were threatened with punishment if she didn't compete for Germany."

The teen listener, glued to his every word, became perplexed. "I don't understand . . ."

"You see," Old John informed, "the Nazis had this all worked out. Gretel complied with their demands, returning home to prepare for the Games. However, just as our ship left New York for Berlin, Gretel was dismissed from the German team."

"How could this happen?"

John explained the Nazis timed it perfectly so the Americans would not have time to protest. He felt, "Hitler played Gretel and Uncle Sam like fiddles."

"So . . . all along the Nazis knew they wouldn't let her compete?"

Old John nodded. "It was Germany tricking the world, pretending to show everyone that the Berlin Games were Jewish-friendly when that was hardly the case."

"What happened to Gretel?"

"She didn't compete, though she'd already jumped previously to the same height that would win a gold medal."

The enraptured teen was beginning to understand. "So, she was forced to come to Berlin for nothing?"

"Yes, but she gained some lifelong American friends . . . including me."

Woodruff closed his eyes, searching his memory bank.

CHAPTER 35

Berlin Stadium, 1936

August 16th was the Berlin Games closing ceremonies. As the orchestra played "*The Games Are Ended*," the crowd joined in the emotional farewell of the athletes, who rocked in time to the music.

There were isolated shouts of "*Sieg Heil!* for Hitler," yet the Fuhrer was being given no role at all in the final exercise. Others took up the cry, and soon the stadium reverberated with the chant, "*Sieg Heil! Unser Fuhrer*, Adolph Hitler, Sieg *Heil!*"

As the stadium cleared, walking away were some athletes who were denied their place in history. American Jews Stoller and Glickman still

1936 Berlin Olympic closing ceremonies, August 16th.

wore looks of shock over having worked so hard to be in the Olympics only to be excluded. However, they felt a little better when seeing the medal count for Black and Jewish athletes.

They studied a list of the African American medalists and also Jewish athletes in the 1936 Olympic Games:

International Black Athletes Olympic medalists:
David Albritton, High jump, silver
Cornelius Johnson, High jump, gold
James LuValle, 400-meter run, bronze
Ralph Metcalfe, 4 x 100-meter relay, gold; 100-meter dash, silver
Jesse Owens, 100-meter, gold; 200-meter, gold; broad (long) jump, gold; 4 x 100-meter relay, gold
Frederick Pollard, Jr., 100-meter hurdles, bronze
Matthew "Mack" Robinson, 100-meter hurdles, bronze
Archie Williams, 400-meter run, gold
Jack Wilson Bantam, weight boxing, silver
John Woodruff, 800-meter run, gold

Jewish Olympic Medalists:
Samuel Balter, USA, Basketball, gold
Gyorgy Brody, Hungary, Water Polo, gold
Miklos Sarkany, Hungary, Water Polo, gold
Karoly Karpati, Hungary, Freestyle Wrestling, gold
Ende Kabos, Hungary, Individual Saber, gold; Team Saber, gold
Irving Matertzky, Canada, Basketball, silver
Gerald Blitz, Belgium, Water Polo, bronze
Ibolya K. Csak, Hungary, High jump, gold
Robert Fein, Austria, Weightlifting, gold
Helene Mayer, Germany, Individual Foil, silver
Ellen Preis, Austria, Individual Foil, bronze
Ilona Schacherer-Elek, Hungary, Individual Foil, gold
Jadwiga Wajs, Poland, Discus Throw, silver

CHAPTER 36

Connellsville, Penna. – under the Woodruff Tree, 2001

John told his teen listener something that would hit home with her. Although the big story was how blacks and Jews became treated, the Asians had a problem amongst themselves.

A Korean runner, Sohn Kee Chung, won the marathon but was denied the honor of collecting the gold medal under either his flag or his name. Japan occupied Korea, and Sohn entered as Kitei Son, the Japanese version of his name. He won the marathon in 2:29.19, more than two minutes faster than Ernie Harper of Britain. Another Korean, Nam Sung Yong, was third.

On the victory stand, the medals became awarded, and the Japanese national anthem began playing. Sohn and Nam, wearing Japan's Rising Sun logo on their uniforms, lowered their heads as the white flag with the rising red Sun became raised.

"It was unendurable, humiliating torture," Sohn had said. "I hadn't run for Japan. I ran for myself and my oppressed Korean people. I couldn't prevent myself from crying. I wished I had never come to Berlin."

There was a bittersweet victory coming for Sohn in 1988, when the Olympics would be in the South Korean capital of Seoul. Sohn carried the Olympic flame on the final lap.

CHAPTER 37

Europe After the Olympics, 1936

Right upon completion of the Games, a group of American runners was invited to race in various cities around Europe. John Woodruff and Jesse Owens were asked to join.

Woodruff to Run in Other Nations Before His Return (Connellsville Courier 1936)

An article read:

Johnny' Woodruff, known to his friends and those fellows on the track team who know him better than anyone else as a retiring sort of youth, found the pomp and glory of being a member of the American Olympic team somewhat uncomfortable.

In a letter written from the Olympic village to his sister Mrs. Genevieve Johnson, who is the keeper for Silas Woodruff, the widowed father of Johnny, the boy says he was glad when their reception was over.

John's letter, in part, follows:

I am writing to let you hear from me. I made the trip over O.K. with a few exceptions. The first days out on the water, I got a little seasick, but I soon got over it. We made several stops, the first in Ireland, but nobody was allowed off the boat. It then stopped at LaHavre, France.

Our first definite stop was in Hamburg, Germany, where we became greeted by the mayor of the city and a large band. We left Hamburg by train to Berlin. When we arrived at Berlin, and the train pulled into the station people were cheering, and a band was playing for us, I was so glad when the reception was over, I don't know what to do. Some things happened. When I return home, I will tell you everything.

The village I am staying in is on the outskirts of Berlin, and it is a beautiful place. The city of Berlin is very beautiful, and I'm going to bring home many pictures of different things.

Coming over on the boat, we were treated like kings. We have all kinds of food we wanted and a variety of it.

I can't tell definitely when I'll be home because I am running other places after the games in Berlin.

The American Olympic team touring Europe split up on whirlwind tours. After the Olympics, Woodruff did some excellent running. In London, he was the anchorman of a US team that set a new World Record at 4 x 880 with 7.35:8. At Dresden, Long John closely won the 800 in 1.52:5 over Kucharski, Harbig third. In Oslo, he performed a surprisingly fast one-lapper in (metric) 46.8, thrashing Roberts of the U.K, Berlin fourth, by a couple of meters. Finally, he posted an impressive 1.50:2 in Paris, running solo most of the time.

Young Woodruff did not make any money for running overseas. The Olympics were for amateurs only, not like today, where they mix in the professional sports stars. He wanted to keep his amateur eligibility, so he could never accept money. If an athlete received more than the allotted two dollars a day, they were not an amateur but a pro.

But for Jesse Owens, he only ran in eight races on tour, and then begged off. Fourteen athletes were in London. Jesse and his Coach Snyder were in the group. They had a couple of days to settle in a hotel in central London and prepare for another exhibition in Scandinavia a few days later.

Jesse Owens was running in several countries and became alerted Scandinavia was next, but he felt drained. After yet another race, a fed-up and tired Jesse talked to his coach, Snyder.

"I've run in eight races, I'm dog tired, lost eleven pounds in the process," said a bemoaned Jesse.

"I know," agreed Snyder. "And you're not making a damned penny for this tour! The AAU's treating all of you athletes like trained seals! Damn, I want to help you here."

"I can't do this anymore. My teammates understand I'm married an' with a child. Gotta look out for my family."

Coach Snyder pulled Jesse aside. "Okay, I'll refuse you flying to Scandinavia. Meanwhile, I'll see what I can do with the union."

CHAPTER 38

Connellsville, Penna. – under the Woodruff Tree, 2001

Old John continued with what happened after the Berlin Olympics. "Jesse disobeying the AAU infuriated Brundage and Cromwell. They rallied to get him banned from all future amateur competitions."

Not helping Jesse Owens had been him telling *The New York Times*, "Somebody's making money somewhere. They're trying to grab everything they can, and we athletes can't even buy a souvenir of the trip."

Jesse Owens refused to run anymore and left Europe. When he arrived back in the US, he became stripped of his amateur athletic status for good.

The lone teen at Woodruff's side realized something. "If you had won your medal today, Mr. Woodruff, you'd be on a Nike commercial making millions!"

"Perhaps, but in my time, two dollars a day was all amateur athletes were allowed to be paid. We didn't even have television. It was a different story."

"After the Olympics," aged John continued, "many significant newspapers reported feeling that the Germans were "back" in the fold of nations and that the Games made them "more humane" again. However, some others thought that the Nazis had succeeded with their propaganda. Three years later, we all would find out the truth."

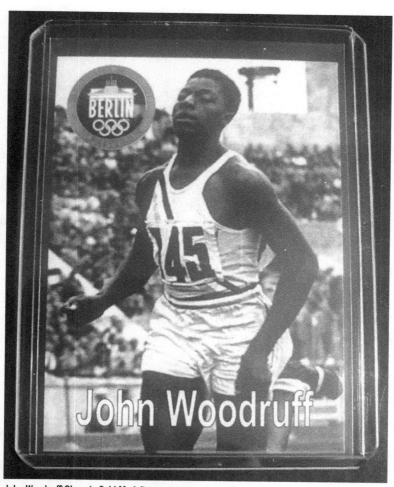

John Woodruff Olympic Gold Medalist custom sports card.

CHAPTER 39

Berlin, Germany, 1936 – After the Olympics

Inside the German Chancellery, Hitler talked to his Reich advisory board, pointing out strategic details on display.

He ordered, "Transform the Olympic village into a training camp."

Throughout Berlin, Anti-Jewish signs were hung back up.

Military movements heightened at the Olympic Village and elsewhere. The *rat-tat-tat* of machine gunfire as the Nazi's, true to their word, came down hard on the prisoners near the Olympic Village.

Several rebellious Jewish prisoners were lined up and shot.

Alongside the Fuhrer was the new stadium designed by Albert Speer. The sheer size of it had Hitler pumped up with delusions of grandeur.

Hitler moved around the stadium artist, rendering like a proud peacock. "We'll take over the Olympics after the Tokyo Games in '40. But after that, they'll reside for all time in our colossal new stadium."

Goebbels had a very satisfactory look. "Our propaganda worked flawlessly. The bonanza showed the world that Germany is rational and tolerant."

Captain Wolfgang Fuerstner, in charge of the Olympic Village and who'd made sure American Woodruff had enough of his favorite pasta, committed suicide with a pistol shot on 19 August 1936, three days after the end of the Games. Füerstner, a career officer, had learned that according to the Nuremberg Laws he was classified as a Jew and was to be dismissed from the Wehrmacht. It was also found that his grandfather was a Jewish convert to Christianity.

CHAPTER 40

Cruise Liner on Ocean, 1936

Several American Gold Medal athletes aboard the deck on the ride home had eighteen-inch tall potted English Oak seedlings.

"What's so special about this tree?" one athlete asked.

Another chimed in, "You're damn, right! Germany spends all that money, putting on a fantastic show an' this mangy shrub is all we get?"

A third athlete came on boldly, "This is what I think of Hitler!"

He tossed his sapling overboard into the sea that swallowed it up. Others did the same with their sprouts.

But not Long John. Again, he read the note attached to his tree: *"Grow to honor the victory! Summon to further achievement!"*

Young Woodruff said to his sapling, "I'm keeping you, little one, to always remind me of beating Hitler."

* * *

The Heroes Return Home, 1936

When Woodruff did return from Europe, he and his teammates became treated with reverence. On the morning of September 3rd, 1936, the United States Olympic team set off on an emotional pageant through New York City. The first stop was a ticker-tape parade down New York City's lower Fifth Avenue.

New York City ticker tape parade for Berlin Olympic heroes upon their return from Europe, Sept, 3, 1936.

The news announcer over the radio speakers said, "This is an amazing and emotional time for Americans. The medal winners became treated like war heroes. Mayor Fiorello La Guardia was presiding their first stop down Broadway."

Conspicuously absent from that great day in New York was President Franklin D. Roosevelt. Neither did he ever call to offer to meet his country's black American champions.

CHAPTER 41

Connellsville, Penna. – under the Woodruff Tree, 2001

"Why wasn't he there?" the teen at John's side asked about FDR. "I mean, you Olympians put Hitler in his place—a victory without bloodshed. Roosevelt should've been there."

"I agree," old John said. "But in his defense, the president back then didn't do what Presidents do today with winning sports teams—inviting the Super Bowl and World Series champs to the White House, Olympic teams, and other college champs as well. Nevertheless, Roosevelt should have at least sent a representative from Washington to show his appreciation."

Many felt Roosevelt did not show up to salute the black athletes because he was involved in an election and concerned about the reaction in the USA's southern states.

Gold Medal winner John Woodruff wore an Olympic blazer and straw top hat and sat in the lineup of Model T convertibles, atop the backseat, and waved to the crowd.

In a cautionary tone, John explained to his teen listener, "However, some black newspapers were very curious of how they would treat blacks now that many of their athletes had shattered the Aryan Supremacy theory. Would it help the blacks to be treated better in their own country?"

Citizens throughout America were waiting breathlessly to see how the great Jesse Owens and the other black Olympic athletes were treated on this swing around the country on a vaudeville tour. Whether they would demand to be treated like all other American citizens in decent hotels or be shunted into black belts or in shanties along the railroad tracks remained to be seen.

Things became evident quickly upon the black gold medal winners' return that there was no invitation to the White House to shake hands with President Roosevelt. That honor was reserved only for the white Olympians.

Old John added, "And what happened to Jesse Owens in New York City poured more salt on the wounds of black Olympic champions."

"What happened to him?" the curious teen asked.

The mature John closed his eyes and remembered.

CHAPTER 42

Waldorf Astoria Hotel, New York, 1936

Jesse Owens was with his mother, both neatly dressed for a ceremony in his honor, but were forced to enter a service elevator.

"Things haven't changed, Mom. After all I've done, we still have to ride in a service elevator."

"Hush now, son. Things'll change, you'll see. And many are proud of you; you remember that."

"If Hitler snubbed me, I don't care," Jesse said with irritation. "But the President of the United States . . . ?"

However, Jesse once again swallowed his pride, turning into the natural performer that he was. Easy and quick to smile plus a humble demeanor, he wooed the sold out crowd with ease. He did not know it at the time, but he would soon learn that he had jumped into another kind of rare atmosphere—one that only a handful of people in every generation are lucky enough to know.

Even though Owens won a mind-boggling four Gold Medals at the Berlin Olympics, it was decathlon winner Glen Morris who received the 1936 James E. Sullivan Award as the top amateur athlete in the United States. Many thought Owens being outright snubbed for the award was segregation at work.

After the Olympics and giving a lot of speeches, Jesse would often be called upon to be a motivational speaker, both in sports and the business world.

In 1976, a U.S. President finally gave Owens long overdue credit. President Gerald R. Ford awarded him the Presidential Medal of Freedom, the highest honor given to civilians in the United States.

CHAPTER 43

Connellsville, 1936

Ten thousand townspeople were there to welcome their champion home. It was the town's biggest parade ever. John would never forget how Mayor Younkin and Dr. Pugia, president of the Connellsville High School Alumni Association, announced that there was going to be a testimonial for him. They and other city officials presented Young Woodruff with the Key to the City. John's University of Pittsburgh coach, Carl Olsen, was there that day, and he pulled aside his prized trackman.

Coach Olsen spoke to John in private. "The athletic department's flooded with questions over information on you. We're unable to answer all these."

Long John gave a sly dig to his coach, "Guess you didn't expect me to do what I did?"

Inside a clothing store, John tried on a suit. A couple of his white boyhood friends observed, including best friend Pete Salatino, who said, "We raised a few dollars from a money pool, finally enough to dress up this big lug!"

"My first suit! Much appreciated, fellas."

Another pair of pants Long John tried on were also too short. "Pete, they're all too short."

"If nothing fits," his chum quipped, "just tell everyone in hot weather you prefer wearin' shorts with your jacket!"

The group laughed along with their friends.

The mayor of Connellsville and most political officials of the Fayette County were there to honor local hero John Woodruff.

The windows of downtown Connellsville became filled with displays of the medals he had won in high school and college, and of there being an afternoon parade. In Fayette Field, a portion of the program was devoted entirely to a testimonial in his honor.

Unlike modern athletes, John received a few dollars from a pocket-money pool. Out of the meager funds collected on his behalf from Connellsville and neighboring Uniontown natives, John bought his first suit of clothes for $17.50.

Oppenheim's, a store in town who had been following Johnny Woodruff's running career along with everyone else, presented him with a complete outfit, all picked from the best in the store. It would include a topcoat, suit, shoes, half a dozen shirts and underwear, one dozen hose, three neckties, three pairs of pajamas, and a pair of gloves.

A local Buick dealer offered Woodruff a car, but he declined to take it because it would have cost him his amateur status.

All of John's boyhood friends were there, just as proud of him as he was proud of them.

Some writers there saw him as 'the fleet-footed boy whose meteoric rise from near obscurity to world fame in three years is another piece of evidence that 'truth is stranger than fiction.'

John's dad was one very proud man. He held his chest out proudly.

According to an *Associated Press* report, it was a Labor Day event that also marked the golden jubilee of the class of 1886 at Connellsville High School.

Connellsville, 2001

The teen listener spoke up, "I read at the library that 'Each community is, in itself, a cornerstone of our nation. And every one of us is but one small, though important block in the foundation in which we live.'" She put her hand on John's shoulder. "You have lain the biggest foundation block of all for Connellsville."

"I did my best," John said humbly. "The Alumni Association and Pop Larew presented me with a fine gold watch, a Lord Elgin," John went on. "It had an engraving on the back, acknowledging my Olympic achievement. I, in turn, gave the city the Olympic oak sapling."

Old John also recalled needing a little precious time alone to visit his mother's grave in Hill Grove Cemetery. He recalled kneeling, touching her tombstone, saying, "Ma, I know you saw me win in the Olympics. I wonder what direction I might've gone if you hadn't told me to give up football?"

"There was nothing to his Olympic medal ceremony as they have to-day," John continued. "No running an extra victory lap, no flag-waving. No high fiving. None of that stuff."

John told of being on the victory stand and presented with a wreath to wear. "I brought that wreath home, but then it dried up and disintegrated," he said. "Some of the gold medalists threw those baby saplings into the ocean, but not me. Or they never bothered to pick them up after being examined in New York by the Department of Agriculture."

"This tree will always remind me of beating Hitler. I felt it would be a nice present for Connellsville," the senior John told the teen under the "adult" Woodruff tree. "For over the years at every track meet, coaches will call attention to this living memorial to the visiting athletes."

CHAPTER 44

Connellsville, Penna. – under the Woodruff Tree, 2001

The teen girl held enraptured by the Olympian John asked, "Did you ever think your baby oak would be so famous when growing up?"

"Not at all," Old John answered. "But look at it now—nearly eighty feet high, a trunk nearly thirteen feet in diameter. It's a piece of Connellsville history."

The Woodruff Tree was one of only a handful of Olympic ones given to American gold medal winners known to still exist in the United States. The main reason was that they had to sit in quarantine for quite some time before entering America. Most were in a sorry state, and some died. But John's sapling survived. Bringing it home, he turned it over to the botany teacher at Connellsville High.

"This teacher was named John Lewis," Woodruff remembered. "We called him Botany John. He worked with the broken tree and nursed it back where it was living because it almost died. After it became relocated from the old Connellsville stadium, it now grows at our present stadium on this Carnegie Field lawn."

John told that for the longest time, the tree, planted here at the stadium, was just another tree not identified as to what it stood for.

"I went to the daily paper and suggested they put some kind of a plaque out there so that the young kids will know the history behind this tree.' So, Driscoll, the *Courier* publisher, did that in 1964. It was dedicated at Commencement exercises."

"Was there some sort of special ceremony when the tree became planted?" his young listener asked.

He shook his head. "No. It was just a tree, I guess. As the years wore on, the symbol of what it stood for took on a living testament sort of meaning."

Now anybody who walked by the tree knew its historical significance, heralding the honor of Connellsville's (and Fayette County's) only Olympic Gold Medalist.

John's audience of one mentioned, "You're not around here much anymore, Mr. Woodruff, but lots of people come to see your tree."

Like the man John Woodruff himself, it was a towering presence at Connellsville High and a symbol of strength and resilience that represented the famed citizen's legacy.

Over the years, people had approached the tree, gathering acorns and planting them wherever the sport of track and field was revered. The Woodruff tree so moved a man from Missouri, and what it stood for, that he had made a special trip to Connellsville for acorns so he could spread them in parts of America far from southwestern Pennsylvania. The Missourian and others revered this oak tree in Connellsville rooted in history, a part of the John Woodruff legend.

The local Shade Tree Commission, and other organizations in the town, called the Woodruff Tree one of the treasures of the community. They were doing whatever they could to keep it as long as they could. Woodruff made them aware of two gold medal trees growing in Southern California. One was the tree awarded for the world-record-setting relay team, on which Owens, Metcalf, Frank Wykoff, and Floyd Draper competed.

"A plaque states that the tree honors Draper, who was declared missing-in-action in World War Two," John said. "Not far away on the California campus was the late Ken Carpenter's gold medal tree."

"Didn't he break the world record in Berlin for throwing the discus?" the teen asked.

"Yes, that's right."

John held up another photo of him running in his Olympic race, his long stride unusually noticeable.

"There was a time when *Pittsburgh Press* sportswriter Jim O'Brien was looking for photographs of me winning the Olympic Gold Medal for use in his book, *"Hail to Pitt,"* John recalled. "But I'd given all the photos I had to Pitt and also to Connellsville High. That's when Elmer C. Leitholf of Baldwin, near Pittsburgh, came to the rescue."

The photo captured Woodruff's tremendous stride.

"Did he take this shot with his camera?" the Old Olympian was asked.

"No." John picked up a letter that accompanied the photo and read: "Leitholf wrote, 'This is a German photo which I retrieved from a bomb-destroyed photoshop in Nuremberg, Germany in 1944.'"

"Eight years after you won the race," a teen brought up.

John nodded, then continued to read from Leitholf's letter, "Unfortunately, I can't read German, but I assume that the attached photo, as well as forty others, including some of Jesse Owens, are equivalent to our 'Bubble gum' cards."

John set aside the note and told the girl that Leitholf had been in Germany with the U.S. Army during World War II.

The teen brought up the tree they were sitting under. "According to the Connellsville Area Historical Society, trees are growing throughout the US that were started from the Woodruff oak."

"That's nice to hear." The Olympian gestured to the big tree that they were underneath.

"Many memories live with this tree," he offered. "It's been said that at the right time of day, you can see the tree's oneness with a black shadow—lengthening in perfect stride."

"Ah, c'mon, sir." The teen thought Mr. Woodruff was pulling her leg.

"Legend has it that way."

The topic of conversation switched to the black athletes.

Old John informed, "Their victories at the Berlin Olympics made some American newspapers confront the hypocrisy of the United States. They had everyone thinking long and hard about the fact that Negroes could be stars in Berlin and second-class citizens back home. And the black press had a field day bringing up how Jesse Owens could order a meal at any restaurant in Hitler's Berlin, but not in President Roosevelt's Washington, D.C. And they were right. Remember me: I had to spend my college days living at a YMCA for blacks, far removed from the white students and their facilities."

The Berlin Olympics had a subtle effect on the thinking in America. The whites, who had never given the racial issue much thought, were opening up their minds on the subject. All of the blacks that won gold medals against the Germans helped their cause, but none more than Jesse Owens. However, like Woodruff, he had his share of bumps after the Olympics. Within hours after winning, he was on his way to losing his amateur athletic status.

"Right after the Olympics," John explained, "I went out for track at Pitt and, of course, the fellow that took care of the locker room there at the old stadium, he told us to put our clothes in baskets in open lockers. We were to be assigned lockers the next day. I put my watch in the pocket of my pants. When I came back to change clothes after practice, it was gone, no doubt robbed by a fellow student."

John's face saddened. "Gone for good. I had it for only two months. I spoke to Coach Olsen, and he said, 'Well, don't make a fuss about it. We'll see what we can do.' But nothing ever happened. I never got the watch, and never heard any more about it."

John did not like how Olsen handled it, and it would not be the last time these two would clash. That watch meant a great deal to him.

"Did you feel racial segregation after you won the medal?" John was asked.

"You would think that after winning gold for my country, that all that Jim Crow stuff was behind me," he answered sadly. "But that wasn't the case. After the Olympics, I returned to Pitt only to suffer the first of several defeats."

How could Woodruff ever forget after his super Berlin achievement going to the famed Charles Restaurant in downtown Pittsburgh to enjoy a meal?

"They wouldn't serve me," he remembered with bitterness. "I said to the restaurant owner: 'I won the gold in the Olympics for America. Guess it doesn't mean a thing to you?' To which the owner replied to me rather awkwardly: 'I'm proud that you did, yes sir. But I also don't want to lose my customers because I now serve negroes.'"

Old John shook his head. "Here I was an Olympic gold medal winner, and it didn't matter. Things were back to normal."

Woodruff told how he returned to the University of Pittsburgh a few days late from Europe to start his classes. "Well, the head of the English department refused to let me begin," John remembered. "I mean, you can't be winning a gold medal and be in class at the same time. Chancellor Bowman was the head of school at the time I went to Pitt, so he must've gotten it straightened out because I know a few days later they let me enter the English course. But that was the discrimination that I ran into when I returned from the Olympic Games."

Coach Olson had Long John work out about three times a week. To develop speed, Johnny honed in on sprints and quarters, and the coach sent him out with the cross-country boys to build stamina.

As to speed, Olson later stated that his new disciple was good for 9.8 at 100 yards and 21 flat at 220 yards. Some track experts felt that no runner, before or since Woodruff, could match his unique combination of speed and stamina that came by as often as Halley's Comet.

"Can you tell about the Naval Academy race that wasn't?" John was asked.

"We had a track meet to run at Annapolis at the Naval Academy," John answered. "Now, here I am, an Olympic champion, and they told the coach that I couldn't run. I couldn't come. So, I had to stay home because of discrimination. That let me know just what the situation was. Things hadn't changed. What made me feel bad was Coach Olsen going along with the decision to race without me. But Coach Van Ely of New York University was told that his black runner Jimmy Herbert couldn't run in that same meet against the Navy, Van Ely didn't like hearing that."

"What did he do?"

"He said, 'If my black runner can't run against Navy, then my team is not running.' And they didn't go to race against Navy. So, you can see why Coach Olsen and I had our problems."

John held a great deal of respect for Coach Van Ely's bold defiance against the Naval Academy. "It was white men like him who helped to change white supremacy attitudes to human equality."

John was not down on all military branches; he did race against Army at West Point. He was a profoundly frustrated man but kept his feelings to himself. "Certainly, I never lost hope of this possibility of change. I knew things had to get better for blacks. I just knew they had to."

He recounted how runner Marty Glickman summarized the racial problem when speaking about Jesse Owens: "He was the idol of the country," Glickman said, "but a week later, he was riding in the back of the bus."

The revered John Woodruff further described the impact of the Berlin Olympics.

Woodruff's powerful stride continues after Olympics for the University of Pittsburgh. (Courtesy of University of Pittsburgh.)

"Over the years, people have said they couldn't imagine what it must have been like for me to enter and win the Olympics with Hitler in attendance in the Nazi Third Reich and endless, powerful, and intimidating *Heil Hitler* arm salutes. They'd never gotten that close glimpse into what we went through. They can't imagine the determination it took for Jesse Owens, me, and all the other blacks to have the guts to rise to the occasion. And the significance of what happened from that point forward."

John continued. "The victories of black Americans at Berlin served as a beacon for all oppressed Americans," he insisted. "And other minority groups as well. I believe we eighteen black athletes truly were the start of the American Civil Rights movement and Jim Crow racism along with the Aryan Supremacy belief."

John told of returning home from Berlin to win every primary race in the country.

"I was never defeated in any major race. *Citius, Altius, Fortius*—Faster, Higher, Stronger—that was the Olympic motto I'd follow to win every race after Berlin."

He told of the IC4As, where he won the quarter and the half, '37, '38, and '39. In the NCAA, the national collegiate championship, John did the same, and in the national IEU meet, he won the half a mile.

"And of course, I ran in the Pan-American games in Dallas, Texas in 1937," he recalled. "Remember, I won the Olympics at the time of 1:52.9.

"About seventy years ago," old John continued, "I had fifteen days in Berlin where my once strong legs ran like the wind. And in less than two minutes in the finals, I became an instant hero to the American people and also the Germans."

John also said that some modern-day athletes do not arrive until the day before their specialty events. They bypassed the opening ceremonies.

"I would never do that," he said. "Missing the opening ceremonies cuts to the heart of what the Olympics are about."

The teen listener heartily agreed, saying that while winning gold medals was very important, the Olympics symbolize more than winning and that the opening ceremonies are the most critical moment of the Games.

"I agree," John said. "Those opening ceremonies—standing proud for your country—are a once-in-a-lifetime opportunity. No amount of money in the world can buy that feeling."

Woodruff went back to telling of another case of racism. One year after he won the gold medal, he was entered in the Pan-American Exposition Games in Dallas. Woodruff was not allowed in the dining car on the train.

It was much the same thing across America, the response from railway guards: "Niggers ain't meant to ride on white trains out here."

John's white running teammates had heard enough.

Don Ohl started an incident by saying to the railway guard, "We're racing in Dallas Stadium tomorrow before a packed house."

Ferrera picked up next, "If our black athletes aren't allowed on your train, and they miss the event, your name will be on newspaper headlines across America!"

Ohl interjected, "You're liable if we don't show up at the track meet."

Ferrara feigned going to a payphone, saying to Ohl, "Maybe we should call the press right now!"

The befuddled railway guard conferred with the train conductor, and they allowed the black athletes to board.

Aboard the train and on their way to Dallas, Woodruff's teammates informed management that if Woodruff could not dine with them, they would not run.

"So, they made a special concession," Woodruff said with a chuckle. "And then, upon arrival, everyone else checked into a hotel. I stayed at the black YMCA, sleeping on a cot in the gymnasium."

Johnny found Texas hospitality humiliating in some respects, as he and the other colored US teamsters were not allowed to stay at the same hotel as their white colleagues. They could not even eat together, and he noticed that in the stadium, there was a small exclusive section for the colored part of the public. On the other hand, the colored athletes of other nations did not have to endure such discriminations.

"It was a long time coming before I would ever stay in a hotel that white folks stayed in," Woodruff said. "However, I was grateful for the whites who stood up for me. Someday, with the grace of God, I just knew sports would be a big help in changing segregation into integration."

In the 800-meter event, white runner Elroy Robinson took the early lead, setting a fast pace (52.5 at midway), with John shadowing him. The Pitt star waited until the last backstretch to commence to let go of one of his withering blasts. The loud cheering for his white adversary seemed to give him an extra lift, and he killed off Robinson's attempts to respond. He crossed the line with seven to eight meters upon him, outclassing the current record-holder. His time: 1.47:8—two full seconds faster than the ratified WR. Robinson got 1.48:8. Dallas ex-prodigy Ross Bush was third, far back.

Then John's expression saddened. "I set the world record in Dallas. But there were several blacks on that team with me. The officials claimed that the five laps to a mile track had been measured within 1/1000 of an inch by the chief engineer of Southern Methodist University, that's the school located there in Dallas. All right, when I set that world's record, it came out in the Dallas papers that they were sure that my record would be accepted as the world's record because the track measured within 1/1000 of an inch."

John shook his head. "Now, I was part of the national track team that was to tour Japan. I left Dallas, went out to the west coast to get on the boat. It came out in the papers about two or three days later, and they said that the record Woodruff had set in Dallas would not be accepted as the World's record because they found the track to be six feet short!"

John sighed. "From 1/1000 of an inch to six feet. Now you know what that was all about; it was just out and out prejudice. They were determined not to give this black boy that race, that record. To this day, I believe it was a discriminatory act on their part. How could they make a mistake of six feet?"

Woodruff became convinced that his time was achieved at the correct distance and was a new World Record, and that the Texas AAU officials found a way to rob him of the record, to avoid giving it to a Negro lad. He firmly believed so up to his death. For whatever reason, Woodruff never again would appear in his show-piece event, the 800, at an AAU competition.

"Did you protest?"

"Yes. I wrote Dan Ferris, who was secretary of the AAU, and registered a complaint. He didn't even have the courtesy to answer my letter. You see, I'd never run a race to set a world's record or anything. I just ran to win. And if it happened to be that I set a record by winning, fine. So this particular time, it was a speedy race, and there was a lot of competition because the man who came in second to me had set a world record at Randall's Island the week before, but I wasn't in that race. They talked me into running the mile, against Glenn Cunningham, the champion miler. So, they tricked me, see?"

"So, what happened?" the teen asked. "That wasn't your race."

"I didn't know that much about the pace of the mile, so I wanted to follow him because of my speed. But they forced me to keep the pace, and I didn't know the mile pace, and I ran myself out. I came in fourth."

Woodruff became selected for another national team going to Japan to compete in the autumn. In the proper match between the two nations, Woodruff emerged victorious at both 400 and 800 meters (48.0/1.58:6), followed home by Bob Young and Charlie Fenske, respectively, anchoring the winning relay quartet. In a later Japanese meet, however, Johnny was caught napping and was narrowly beaten by a hometown runner, in a slow time and on a muddy track.

John's keen memory recalled Elroy Robinson from Fresno State, California, who ran the half a mile. In the week before, John had beaten him in Milwaukee. Robinson ran the half-mile in 1:49.6, and that was a new world record.

". . . But I wasn't in the race," John repeated. "See, I was in that mile race, so it came out in the papers. They said, 'Well, if Woodruff would have been in that race, Robinson would have lost.' And that was written by Jess Abrams. That set things up for a perfect race in Dallas in the Cotton Bowl. Regardless of where we would've run, it would have been a good race because of the psychology that developed."

When they got to Dallas, Elroy Robinson was a front-runner, and he jumped right ahead. "He ran first, and I ran second for the first lap. When we hit the first turn of the second lap, which is the last lap, I pulled up beside him, you see and then coming down the backstretch, we battled it out. And then I broke and came on in to set that new world record. Now he finished about twelve yards behind me—you know he'd set the world record the week before. I ran 1:47.8. He ran about 3 or 4 seconds slower than my race. I used to know exactly what he ran, it was 1:48 something, but that's how it turned out. I set the record, but they decided they'd come up with something that wasn't right. But a track six feet short? No way."

"Did you ever feel like quitting in the face of discrimination?"

John answered, "I mean, all that work for nothing. The fastest race I ever ran, only to lose a world record. Instead of complaining, I dug deep into my character and kept on racing."

CHAPTER 45

A track meet after the 1936 Olympics

At a track meet in Ohio later on, John Woodruff was surprised to be greeted by Jesse Owens in street clothes. They warmly embraced each other as fans took photos of them before the Olympian greats moved off for privacy.

"Heard about you were robbed at the Pan Ams," Jesse eventually brought up.

Young Woodruff shook his head. "A chief engineer at Southern Methodist University measured the track to be within 1/1000 of an inch before the race. But two days after I won, they suspiciously re-measured the distance and said it was six feet short!"

"They all need eyeglasses!" Jesse said, displeased.

"Those boys got their heads together, and decided they weren't going to give a black man a white man's record. That was my fastest run ever—like my feet weren't touching the ground."

"Did you file a complaint with my good friends who hate me at the AAU?"

"I did, but never heard back," John said.

"No big surprise," grunted Jesse. "He was on Brundage and Cromwell's side to get me barred from the amateur track. That tore a big hole in me."

"I feel for you, Jess."

"At twenty-four, my time as a serious athlete is washed up."

Young John asked, "What about those business offers after your Olympic golds?"

"Nothin' but hot air. Now I'm forced to make a buck by turning into a circus act. I even went against a racehorse in Havana."

John could not contain a chuckle. "You win?"

"Yep. It sure felt good racing on cinders again! Some are sayin' it's degrading for an Olympic champ to run against a horse. But what am I supposed to do? Four gold medals, but you can't eat gold medals!"

"I hear you."

"Now I got offers to run against trains, motorbikes, baseball players with a head start, and a greyhound dog. Being treated like a freak, an animal, but hell, I need the dough."

"You're a living legend," Woodruff emphasized. "Something good will happen."

"So far, I'm a poor legend. Coming home to the parades, that's been it. Have to fight to earn a living and support my family."

Jesse told of once using his Olympic jacket to keep warm while working as a street sweeper.

John put a hand on Jesse's shoulder. "I'll find a way to help you."

Jesse smirked. "You, an amateur jock allowed only two dollars a day, wants to help me?"

"I know but—"

"Help by setting another 800 record—one they can't take away from you. Even if I gotta come to measure the track myself!"

Long John shook his head. "For you, I'll give it my best shot."

CHAPTER 46

Berlin, Germany, 1937

Adolf Hitler was in the Architect Design Room of Albert Speer. They stood in front of a seven-foot-high model of the new German Stadium that Hitler had plans to build.

Speer explained, "Every detail is accurate, *Mein Fuhrer.* It will accommodate four hundred thousand spectators, the largest stadium ever built, even bigger than the Circus Maximus in Rome, built to hold 150,000 to 200,000 people. Even larger than the Great Pyramid Cheops in Egypt."

Speer went on to say the Great Stadium would be horseshoe-shaped. The sheer massiveness of the Great Stadium would be made mostly of granite—pink on the exteriors, white for the three hundred-plus feet high stands.

Hitler was amazed while studying the colossal stadium. "Its design is truly unparalleled in the history of the world."

"We'll lay the cornerstone on September 9th of this year."

Hitler solemnly shook hands with him. "Albert Speer, this is the greatest day of your life!"

Speer became caught off guard. "No, not today, *Mein* Fuhrer, but when the building becomes finished."

They shared an uncomfortable laugh.

Speer told that the structure would be called *The Great Stadium*.

Hitler liked the name immensely and asked about another building about to be erected. "How is the German Embassy in Washington progressing?"

Speer displayed a rendition of it to Hitler, adding: "The contractor to oversee the building project will be your choice, Avery Brundage."

Hitler nodded in approval. "His sympathy for the Nazi cause has helped us tremendously. Did you know that the fraternity Brundage is a member of excludes all Jews?"

CHAPTER 47

Connellsville, Penna. – under the Woodruff Tree, 2001

John finished his collegiate career at the University of Pittsburgh in addition to being a member of the campus Alpha Phi Alpha fraternity, the first black fraternity in America. When Penn Relays officials decided to start a Wall of Fame to commemorate the meet's 100th anniversary in 1994, Woodruff, who won eight races running anchor legs in three appearances, earned more votes than any other candidate.

"We won the IC4As track meet here at home," Woodruff added. "I won my two races in the quarter and the half, for three years."

He won the NCAA for three straight years, 1937-1939, and also won up at Dartmouth College indoors in 1:46.7.

"That was a world record at that particular time," Woodruff went on, proud of the achievement. "And I won the national AAU meet in Milwaukee, Wisconsin. I won every major race in the country when I came back from the Olympics."

However, he came to love the excitement of racing at the great Penn Relays and Millrose Games with a baton in his hand. He led his Pitt team to a new meet record in the sprint medley event.

Arthur Daley of the *Times* wrote, "John Woodruff anchors Pitt to three wins and two meet records, coming from behind in each race. With that running marvel Ol' John Woodruff unreeling one of his smooth anchor legs, Pitt won the sprint medley championship that had seemed ordained for it from the start."

Woodruff confirmed being victorious at nine Penn relay races, anchoring the 4 x 800-meter run. Long John was always the anchorman because he was the fastest and the strongest. "I was never defeated."

Then he caught himself. "I take that back . . . the week before the try-outs in Princeton, Charlie Beetham, a great half-miler from Ohio State, beat me at Princeton. And then I was second in Japan in 1937, when I went over there with the track team."

However, the way athletes traveled in John's day was an ordeal compared to how athletes went today: thirty-six-hour rides in stuffy cabins of propeller-driven planes or boat rides across oceans with heaving waters inviting sea sickness. Often, they were travel-weary when running a race.

How could old John ever forget on that particular day it rained heavily, and of course, his stride became messed up. John chuckled. "This little Japanese fellow, you know a little fellow, went right through that water and mud, and he defeated me."

John recalled the soggy ground, adding, "And then I got sick. They wanted to take out my tonsils. I had a bad case of tonsillitis. When I came back to the University, I went to the hospital there in Pittsburgh, and they operated on me. That was my very first operation, but I've had many since then."

"When you were running for Pitt after the Olympics, did you think about going to the Olympics again?"

"Well, yes, I did," the legendary runner answered. "I felt I had a chance at winning another Gold Medal, and of course, I now had more experience. That would've been at the end of my collegiate years, 'cause I finished in '39, and the Olympics were supposed to be in '40. But it was disappointing, for I would have been in my prime in 1940. It wasn't too disappointing because, after all, I'd gone in '36 and took home gold."

Woodruff Initially Hated Running Indoors, But Not the Fans

Long John and indoor running did not combine well. New York track experts surmised, ". . . He wobbles badly on the turns, is late in beginning to lean to the inside approaching them, his feet nearly pull him over the bunk . . ."

Woodruff did not particularly like running indoors because of the hard surfaces and all the cigar and cigarette smoke.

Long John admitted to his listener of having a talk with himself as he lined up at the start of the run. "Here we go again, Johnny, just like as a boy and that train kicking up dirt and gravel into my face. These big city boys got all kinds of tricks, so get ready."

However, it began just like John's heroic Olympic run. He became pocketed right away but this time he tried to pass them on the rail lane, but there was no opening.

What to do next? John thought. Once again, John fell back into last place. From there he went around the field. At halfway, he was fifth. It was then that John summoned his engines. He began picking off runners, one after the other, and burst into the lead on the last turn.

John recalled, "I learned from experience never to let up, never to think the race was over until I crossed the finish line. And it proved true. My eyes almost popped out of my head when I saw Borck draw alongside me. The audacity of this runner! There was no loafing now, and I went to town. I was off again in flight, that wondrous zone that has to be experienced to be fully appreciated. I glided and glided, seemingly weightlessly and opened up a gap of six yards to win."

He took the Pitt team to a new meet record in the sprint medley event.

John Woodruff also became a favorite at Madison Square Garden. His clashes with John Borican became great gate pullers.

Another worthy foe of John in half-mile races was Howie Borck, who admitted that "Woodruff was one of the greatest runners ever, and that someday John is going to run, and when he does he's going to drive that 880 record so far out of sight that we'll never find it again!"

John recalled what it was like working out at Pitt on the track field when interrupted by a white teammate seeking pointers in middle distance running. John was most accommodating in helping any way he could.

"We have different styles," John explained to the runner. "I'm mostly natural, and you have a lot of technique. Maybe we can learn a little from each other."

The teammate lit up, honored with being asked to advise a gold medal winner.

After practice, Coach Olsen, with several teammates in tow, gave John the good news. "You've been voted the new team Captain," Coach told John. "Do a good job for us."

Long John was deeply touched. "I'll do my best, Coach."

Teammates huddled around their new captain, backslapping him.

After practice, when the runners were alone, runner Don Ohl suggested, "Let's go to a bar and celebrate!"

"Not a good idea," said runner Ferrera. "The only place allowing blacks is a real dive. Maybe we can go to—"

"Thanks, guys," John broke in. "But I have to study for an exam. Perhaps it's best, and I see you all tomorrow."

As their new captain left, the others bemoaned John's situation.

Don Ohl: "Life isn't fair for John."

"No, kidding," Ferrera added. "He comes to Pitt with only 25 cents to his name, can't live on campus—"

"—But becomes our biggest track star ever," Ohl added. "Yet can't go in a place to have a beer."

An excited Long John walked across campus, talking to himself. "You were right, mama, yes, you were. You didn't raise a son to be a loser. *Captain* of the team in 1937! Who would've thought it could happen? My white teammates are respecting me—what a great feeling!"

John stopped to take a campus newsletter from a pile and hurriedly flipped the pages.

His shoulders slumped after reading through a list of names and not seeing his name.

Old John told the news: "Pitt snubbed me from their first sports Hall of Fame. That omission hurt. Here I was the only Olympic champion in the history of the school at the time. Athletes from several sports made it, but not me. Those guys brought national recognition to Pitt. I brought the school *international* recognition."

Young John crumpled the newsletter, tossing it into a garbage can.

"Instead of complaining, I dug deep into my character and kept on racing."

On Friday, April 30, 1938, at the 44th Penn Relays Carnival in Philadelphia, and Woodruff made up a deficit to anchor Pitt's sprint medley unit (Frank Phil, Al Ferrara, and Dick Mason) to a world record 3:34.5 time, as he ran the 880 in 1:49.9. The following day, he anchored the half-mile relay team (the same foursome) to victory, and then the mile unit (Allen "Red" McKee replaced Mason on the third slot) to victory. On May 27th of the same summer, Woodruff won the 440 and 880 in the IC4A track and field meet, equaling the college mark of forty-seven seconds for the 440.

"Penn was the most exciting meet I've ever run," Old John exclaimed. "When I ran there for Pitt, I anchored three relay winners a year for three years. It was more thrilling winning at Penn than winning in the Olympics."

His performances in the Penn Relays events were truly magnificent. He became the hero of the meet. John was instrumental in Pitt winning three events, two of which in a meet record, and the process, he was timed in fine 21.5 - 47.4 - 1:49.9. The *New York Times* wrote that "he is a wonder; that is about all there is to it . . ."

In 1938, they wanted John to run in a track meet in Europe. "Well, I decided I wasn't going to Europe," John voiced. "I went back to Pitt because I wanted to graduate with my class. I got a job with the buildings and grounds crew, and I went to school. And I worked on some courses that I had to take in the fall. There was one course in statistics I took that summer because it wasn't as hard, and that helped me. So, as a result of going to summer school, I only had to take eleven credits for each semester my senior year. It made it easy for me, so that's what I did."

John confessed that it was tough to pass up that European tour, but he remembered the vow he made to himself upon entering the Univeristy of Pittsburgh: *if I didn't make it in school, he wasn't going back home to Connellsville.*

"You see, I had something to prove to myself, and for my race, a fire in my stomach," he added. "That's why I passed up summer in Europe."

In his senior season of 1939, Woodruff repeated his IC4A and NCAA titles, and anchored three winning relay teams at the Penn Relays. The Pitt teams, which he captained in 1939, were undefeated in dual meets.

"In high school," old John made known, "I was primarily a miler but became tempted to try it seriously. Yet, first, I wanted to go after another Olympic 800 gold at the 1940 Games. After that, running the mile would necessitate a change in training technique, but it won't affect my stride. It's all a matter of timing, and I feel that I can time my race right, doing a pretty good mile. Unfortunately, the war was to interfere with my plans."

John brought up a humorous story of hating to run indoor track because his long stride was cut down by the lack of straightaway runs and having to deal with the multitude of curves on the boarded wood track.

"I hated Madison Square Garden," Woodruff continued. "At that time, it was in its old location on 49th Street and Eighth Avenue."

Nevertheless, he won the Millrose Games gold there and was very proud of himself.

In collegiate dual meets, Woodruff's powers became utilized at a maximum. Sometimes he started at the 440/880/mile in the same afternoon and won them all, besides anchoring the relay team for good measure. Yet he was hardly sent up to the shot-put circle anymore. Ironically a sportswriter commented that John was doing about everything except collecting tickets at the gate.

CHAPTER 48

Indoor Track Meet – Madison Square Garden, 1938

Long John was in another race at the Garden running on the famed circular indoor track. Cigar and cigarette smoke from many cheering fans permeated the arena with a blanket of haze.

In between breaks, Long John had a surprise guest who lived in New York City—Marty Glickman. He came down on the track when Long John was waiting for his turn to compete. The two gave each other a bear hug before sitting in empty chairs.

"Never thought I'd race indoors," admitted Long John. "But it helps me keep the competitive edge."

"Watch out for these tricky New Yorkers ready to get you all tangled up."

"I've learned all about that. Took a spill the last time here, picked splinters out of my legs for weeks!"

John showed scratches and bruises on his legs. "But I got to admit I'm starting to love the excitement, the crowd cheering so close you can almost touch 'em. What's up with you?"

"After I graduate from Syracuse, I might give pro football a shot," Glickman made known. "Or use my gift of gab and give sports announcing a try. Gotta make money somehow."

"You're fast enough to race against horses with Jesse!" Long John chided.

They shared a laugh over that one.

Long John turned severe. "I'm keeping in shape for the upcoming Olympics. Hope Hitler doesn't interrupt things."

"Oh, speaking of that mustached infection," Glickman said, "Gretel Bergmann, the German Jew high jumper, has immigrated to America! She's now living in New York City, married to Bruno Lambert, a physician."

A big grin overtook Long John. "Great! I'm so glad for her that she left Germany."

"That gal's determined to reclaim the world high jump record."

"I'd love to see her stick it to Adolf. Looking forward to meeting Mrs. Gretel Bergmann-Lambert."

"Wouldn't that be something," Glickman beamed. "Win a medal or two for America!"

Ironically, upon Gretel becoming an American citizen, she promptly won national championships in the high jump and shot put. She repeated as national champion in the high jump in 1938. Little did John know at the time that when Gretel Bergmann-Lambert and he would finally meet they would keep in touch with each other the rest of their lives.

CHAPTER 49

Connellsville, Penna. – under the Woodruff Tree, 2001

The aged Woodruff collected his thoughts.

John told of running in more races, his legs stretching into foreverland. "In '39, I graduated from Pitt but continued racing in events in '40. I set a world-record at Dartmouth College, but once again, it wouldn't go in the record books."

"Here we go again!" the teen said, riled. "What did they find wrong this time?"

"The track was ruled too oversized at 240 meters—longer and had fewer turns than the typical indoor track."

With Woodruff out of college competition, there were not many essential meets outdoors for Long John to compete. Besides, the Olympics were looking more and more like they might not occur, which had John feeling utterly disappointed. He competed sparsely.

The track enthusiasts in his Connellsville hometown planned a match race between him and Borican for the end of April. It fell through. John stepped the distance in 1:55.2, with Curtis Giddings as a replacement in second. Two weeks later, however, it did happen. On the track of a "colored" college at Greenboro, N.C., they clashed. The pair of them established a ding-dong battle in the last stretch and finished neck to neck. John was judged the winner by inches. Time: 1.54:5, on a slow course.

On June 1, they again tangled, this time at 3/4 mile, on a soggy track at Bridgeton, New Jersey, Borican's hometown. The outcome was hardly satisfactory to them, neither to the public who were there to see Borican win. Blaine Rideout, a Texas miler, had more steam at the end, and John's finish missed its target by a short yard. Borican came in another yard later. Time: 3:12.2.

"The winter of '40," old John said with emphasis, "I had one last shot to keep a promise I made."

CHAPTER 50

Compton Invitational Track Meet, California, Winter 1940

Long John was again crouched at the starting line, saying to himself, "If the Olympics are canceled, this could be my last shot to set a record. Here it goes, Jesse Owens. This one's for you."

The runners took off with Long John looking akin to a kingly horse, legs corded with muscle that rocketed him down the track. Eyes locked on the finish line, he charged forward.

Leading the race from the shot and up to the tape, he produced a new 1:48.6 national record. The performance placed him in second place on the year's world list, headed by Harbig's 1:47.8. A Stanford miler/half-miler, Paul Moore, was tagging John in the race until the latter stretched his legs at the finish, still appearing quite fresh. He left the unexpected challenger some four meters behind at the post. John's record was not to be equaled until twelve years later, by his successor as Olympic champion, Mal Whitfield.

The scoreboard displayed: Winner John Woodruff - 1:48.6 – New American Record

CHAPTER 51

Connellsville, Penna. – under the Woodruff Tree, 2001

The aged Woodruff took on a sad expression. "Unfortunately, that was the end of my running career, at twenty-four years old."

His listener under the tree was miffed. "What about the upcoming Olympics?"

"It wasn't meant to be."

"But running was your life. How could you live without it?"

Old John closed his eyes.

"After getting my bachelor's degree at Pitt, I went to NYU for my Masters in Sociology. I lived with my sister Margaret in New Rochelle, who was working at the Harlem Hospital. I commuted to Manhattan to pull a shift as an elevator operator in a department store—from 6:30 A.M. to 4:30 P.M., six days a week. I rose at 5 A.M. to start each day. Those were long days that required a lot of determination. But you see, by then, I'd begun focusing on another goal."

"Just as I did in track," he continued, "I painted a picture in my mind of what I would like to do or be. And one of those images was me going up in front of the university and receiving my diploma. I cared so much about that image of me graduating that I did all I could to make it happen."

Old John recalled, "Most of my studying was on trains and when operating the elevator. You see, I had a surreal vision of someday becoming "Professor" John Woodruff, in jacket and tie with a textbook in hand.

I set my sights on becoming a college professor. Motivating youths to expand their minds sounded very rewarding, indeed."

John told of his love for reading that stayed with him all his life. Combined with his unique life experiences, he felt he had something to truly offer students that were hungry to learn.

However, John told the teen about Japan bombing Pearl Harbor on December 7, 1941.

"But life takes its turns when it wants to," Old John continued. "It doesn't ask what we want; it just gives, and sometimes it takes. The war waging in Europe canceled the '40 Tokyo Olympic Games. I didn't even attend my graduation ceremonies. A friend picked up my degree."

"You went off to war?" asked John's listener.

Mr. Woodruff nodded. "I joined the Army in 1941. I didn't know where the war would take me, but I was determined to do my share to beat Hitler again."

CHAPTER 52

A Peaceful Man Goes to War

The 1940 Games were scheduled in Japan—Sapporo for the Winter Games, Tokyo, for the summer. But Japan and China went to war in 1938, and the Japanese cities withdrew. An incredible period began, in which the IOC became the ostrich of the sports world and refused to believe what it was seeing.

Feeling it should stay out of world politics, the IOC moved the Winter Games to St. Moritz, Switzerland, and the Summer Games to Helsinki, Finland. That was not the end. The Swiss argued over IOC rules that classify ski instructors as professionals, so the IOC moved the Winter Games again, this time to Garmisch-Partenkirchen, Germany. That decision came in June 1939, after Germany invaded Austria.

On September 1, 1939, Hitler's armies invaded Poland, and two days later, Britain and France declared war on Germany.

John remembered saying to news reporters back then, "He followed his plan as outlined in *Mein Kampf.* People thought Hitler was a fool, but he carried out his program to the letter as outlined in his book."

Within a week, after vowing vengeance against Japan's attack on Pearl Harbor on December 7, 1941, America joined the Allied Forces in Europe and declared war on Germany and Italy.

Woodruff enlisted in the US Army in January 1941, training at a unit stationed at Fort Ontario, Oswego, New York.

Long John did not give up the sport of track running entirely, saying, "In the military I made a few track performances, being persuaded by fellow service athletes to participate. My debut for the coast artillery track team of Oswego, New York, ended badly. At the indoor AAU championship, running a sprint medley relay leg, I tripped and fell. Yet at the Penn Relays, my appearance as a member of the artillery team at the end of April was a success."

Lt. Woodruff ran his 440 leg in 49.5 seconds and received a loud ovation, the most significant hand of all. He said that he had trained for two weeks to get there. In 1942, he also entered for the same relay for Camp Edwards. Later in the year, he was sent to the Pacific, being stationed in Hawaii for some length of time.

"I served in the South Pacific in a segregated unit, as all units in the war were," Woodruff informed. All of his services were served in the Pacific, beginning from Hawaii, Okinawa, Korea, and the mainland of Japan.

Because of being a college graduate, he entered the army as a second lieutenant but flew up the ranks. However, things were not great for black soldiers.

In 1943, "Captain" John Woodruff, in military uniform, addressed Black soldiers in the South Pacific Islands.

"My mission is to get your sorry asses in top shape so you can survive over here, defeat our enemy, and get home in one piece."

One soldier whispered to another, "What's the hurry? Back home, whites are still gonna treat us like dogs."

Even though there were proposals by the NAACP urging the creation of a volunteer army division "open to all Americans irrespective of race, creed, color, or national origin," it did not happen. And that was the least of it. Black soldiers had a war raging on two fronts—one against the enemy and another against whites in the American uniform.

JOHN Y. WOODRUFF
Army
South Connellsville

Jim Crow became practiced at just about every American camp. Blacks had to sit at the back of transport buses, in the back of theaters, in the back of just about everything. Black officers were routinely insulted, and black soldiers often lived in vastly inferior quarters. Even their training for war was inferior to that of the white soldier.

President Roosevelt had promised that black military strength would be 10 percent of the total military, reflecting the proportion of blacks in the United States generally. But three-quarters of blacks in the US armed forces were assigned into service and supply units. Though much of their duty was menial, much was essential.

The following year Woodruff married. Among the guests at John's 1942 wedding to his first wife, Hattie Mae Davis, was good friend Jesse Owens. The Woodruff's had two children, Randelyn (Randy) Gilliam, now a retired teacher living in Chicago and John, Jr., a trial attorney in New York. Five grandchildren and three great-grandchildren also survive him.

John ascended the military ranks to captain in Artillery. He was stationed in Japan and Okinawa in 1942-1945. He commanded two battalions, one integrated and was executive officer for five artillery battalions. However, John, like most blacks in the service, hit some rough segregation spots in the army.

Black soldiers still had to move to the back of the convoy bus when white soldiers entered to ride in front.

White soldiers lived in clean barracks and black soldiers housed in near slum quarters.

POW camps featured American officers smoking cigarettes and relaxing with German uniformed officers.

It has become documented that German prisoners of war became treated much better than the black soldiers of the United States.

While John was at war, his adopted town of Pittsburgh continued fighting it on the home front. The determined man told of the black newspaper *The Pittsburgh Courier* having strong support for blacks during World War II.

They spearheaded the successful "Double V" (double victory) campaign. Beginning in the paper's February 7, 1942 edition and continuing weekly until 1943, the double V campaign demanded that African Americans who were risking their lives abroad receive full citizenship rights at home. The newspaper printed articles, editorials, Double V photographs, and drawings, and even designed a recognizable Double V sign to promote the campaign. Many other black newspapers endorsed the campaign as well, making it a nationwide effort.

The Americans were winning the war, with help from talented pilots and bombers like the Tuskegee Airmen, skilled generals like Gen. Benjamin O. Davis Sr. and women working in factories back home in America. The other victory stands for a win at home. This V would be a victory over prejudice and discrimination towards people of different races or colors. James G. Thompson sent a letter to the *Pittsburgh Courier* stating his ideas for a new campaign. He ended up being one of the idea-makers of the Double V Campaign, and in it, he expressed many of his concerns and ideas about racism and its solution.

CHAPTER 53

South Pacific Islands, 1944

Officer Woodruff was overseeing his unit of Black soldiers setting up Base Camp, where he also went through drills with them.

The Army's newest "Lieutenant Colonel" John Woodruff took an oath that year and donned the new shoulder straps signifying his rank at his promotion ceremony.

He served in the South Pacific in a segregated unit. Being a college graduate, he entered the army as a Second Lieutenant but rose rank to Lieutenant Colonel. In 1941, there were only twelve African American officers in the military. He was one of them.

John often ran alone in military uniform to keep in shape, for the runner in Long John Woodruff still had a dim dream. If the war had ended soon, he thought perhaps that he could run in the '44 Olympics. But it was not to be with the war still raging, the Games became canceled again. And life changed; having been at war puts things in perspective. He became determined to be the best military officer possible.

Many sportswriters were convinced that if the World War had not taken away his running career, he would have become the long-awaited "four-minute" miler instead of Roger Bannister in 1954.

After World War II was over, soldier Woodruff thought long and hard of being denied his prime years on the running track. It stung him, for sure, but he never forgot would could sting more—Germany or Japan conquering the United States. That competition had to come first, as it did for a lot of great professional athletes who lost the prime years in their sport due to serving in the armed forces.

CHAPTER 54

April 30, 1945

Reading the bold, full-paged newspaper headlines of the suicide of Adolf Hitler, Captain Woodruff had his mouth agape. It signaled the final nail in the coffin for the Axis Powers in World War II.

Soldier Woodruff rubbed his eyes and looked at something in the distance that only he saw, capped by heavy breathing. "Nearly seventy

Allegedly the last picture of Adolf Hitler before he committed suicide on April 30, 1945 (right) and his adjutant Julian Schaub looking at the ruins of the Reich chancellery.

World War II damage to Berlin, 1945.

The fall of Nazi Germany.

million people died because of you," Woodruff thought. "And for what? You killed yourself after you started losing."

After being discharged in 1945, Woodruff returned to service during the Korean War and finally left in 1957 as a Lieutenant Colonel. He was the battalion commander of the 369th Artillery, later the 569 Transportation Battalion New York Army National Guard and Officer in Charge and Control Armory in Harlem, New York City.

CHAPTER 55

The Racial War Continues, 1950s

Compared to other blacks, Woodruff did not feel mistreated. However, it became known that some were treated worse than enemies.

Black groups began to rally for democracy, coming home to use the Declaration of Independence, the Bill of Rights, and the Constitution to nourish the frail shoots of civil rights. They wanted to make sure that black soldiers would never again fight and die for a country that did not treat them like Americans.

———

Woodruff and the Korean War, 1950–1957

John's career as a soldier continued, serving his country in the Korean War. While helping to protect his country, he also had to fight racial discrimination from his countrymen. He became a captain commanding a segregated unit and later helmed a non-segregated group.

While enduring criticism and persecution, Woodruff rose to the top.

John recalled: "It became obvious quickly that some white soldiers wanted nothing to do with a black leader, no matter how good he was. I knew, just like back home in Connellsville, or with my college and Olympic track members, if I stayed righteous and honest, treating everyone the way I wanted to be treated, it'll somehow work out. Now I had to once again put that theory to the test."

———•———

Korea 1952

Lieutenant Colonel John Woodruff had ordered his "integrated" unit on reconnaissance over an open field. Things changed during the Korean War. Truman integrated black and white soldiers into the armed forces, and he was a part of it.

Lt. Colonel Woodruff pointed to a small group of mixed-race soldiers. "I need you, Joes, to run under the tree canopy out there and hunker down. Hump ass those four-hundred yards, nut to butt."

Some soldiers hemmed and hawed, especially a disgruntled, cocky white one who did not budge.

"I don't take orders from a black officer!" he said defiantly to his superior.

Woodruff got in the soldier's face. "There are two ways to handle this. I write up papers and dispatch you to the brig where you'll be a latrine queen. Or you can follow orders. What's it going to be?"

Lt. Colonel Woodruff circled him, sizing him up. "How about this," he offered. "I'll race you pissin' and moaning grunts. If I win, you follow orders without giving lip. Your call, soldier."

Several white soldiers egged others to take up the challenge.

The defying white soldier said, "You're on!" Woodruff and the white soldier limbered up before getting into a starting position.

Another soldier gave the "Go" signal. Lt. Colonel Woodruff tore off, leaving the defiant soldier and other white ones trailing far behind.

All the soldiers, black and white, stared in awe over their speedy ranking officer.

CHAPTER 56

Connellsville, Penna. – under the Woodruff Tree, 2001

Old John's eyes opened. "I broke protocol and took a chance. A part of me wanted to show these white guys that I was better than them. Leftover resentment, I guess from the Olympics."

"Well, I'm glad you did," the girl said. "That soldier needed to be taught a lesson."

"I was wrong, honey," admitted Old John. "War isn't a game. People die and suffer tremendously. It's not a place to satisfy one's whims."

"I know."

"But you don't know that those irritated white soldiers turned out to be some of my best. And for many of the black soldiers, it gave hope that they weren't fighting and dying for a country that didn't treat them like Americans."

"Perhaps so," the listener went on. "But why am I not surprised that you were a leader in war just like you led your white teammates when named captain of Pitt's track team?"

Elder John considered that. "Well, you may have a point there. I never asked to be a leader in anything, just worked with all the others to be the best that I could be. I guess that mindset has a way of rubbing off on other people."

———————

In 1956, right before Woodruff retired from military service, he made it back home. It was the 150th birthday of Connellsville. Thousands were paying homage to the *Sesquicentennial 150.*

John Woodruff helped Mayor Daniels, apply a flaming torch to the Eternal Light Monument right at Route 119 and North Pittsburgh Street.

The lighting of the flame was in the spirit of the ancient Greek Olympic Games, and John Woodruff carried the Olympic torch. It had already been ignited at Gettysburg National Park's Eternal Flame and brought to Connellsville, covering the final lap.

Woodruff had led the old fashioned torch-light parade from Brimstone Corner and to its way to North Apple Street. With his athletic career long over and his service in the military just ending, John was in the procession that included the Keystone Cops, Molinaro's Band, and the parade committee. Others in the march included Joint High School runners, 250 torchbearers, Ham and Gravy group with stagecoach and goat, the New Haven Hose Company Band, Shades of the Past Cavalcade Characters, the Mount Pleasant Drum and Bugle Corps Zundeliers, Troutman's girls, and Volunteer Police. The parade, always with members of the city's fraternal and patriotic organization, even traveled along the Youghiogheny River.

The first fifty years brought many people to Connellsville when coal became discovered in the area. In this heyday, it was estimated to have a population of 22,000, more than double its current population. Connellsville would be genuinely remembered for the position it held as the world's coke center.

The *Sporting Image* wrote an article at this time called the "Unsung Heroes of the Olympics." They said of John Youie Woodruff: "In civilian life the selfless manner in which Woodruff applied his energies for the good of society was humbling and for a man of his achievements, beyond the call of duty as many may have seen it. It is as if there were some ethical blueprints in his DNA to place himself in the most difficult social situations and try and do some good, a missionary of sorts. He seemed to have acted this way throughout his life, and he never shied away from the challenges of helping people in difficult social circumstances. In his later career, he targeted associations whose remit was charitable, educative, and ultimately social or rehabilitative; always taking an interest in others and caring for their progress in life, wherever they came from. John fulfilled his mission across a number of roles."

CHAPTER 57

The Life and Times of John Woodruff, Post War

John considered a military career until he retired, after which he planned to return to New York. After leaving military service in 1957, he lived in New Rochelle in Westchester County, New York, and in Hightstown and Edison, New Jersey; East Windsor, New Jersey; and Sacramento, California.

In 1968, John accepted a job in Indiana to manage residents enrolled in the US Job Corps, a federal anti-poverty program aimed at helping at-risk youth. Ultimately the move split up the Woodruff family and led to divorce.

In 1970, Woodruff remarried to Rose Ella King Woodruff. Once when John was going to Georgia to visit her, a white Georgia University track coach came to pick him up at the airport. That was unheard of back then in the South. Picking him up was a sign of respect for what he did on the athletic field. The bond that athletes form was strong.

Woodruff coached young athletes and officiated at local and Madison Garden track meets. He also worked as a teacher in New York City, New York City's Children's Aid Society, a special investigator for the New York Department of Welfare, a recreation center director for the New York City Police Athletic League, a parole officer for the state of New York, a salesperson for Schieffelin and Co., and an assistant to the Center Director for Edison Job Corps Center in New Jersey. He also was a Sunday school teacher in a Baptist Church when living in New Jersey.

The mild-mannered, disciplined, and strapping John Woodruff also became more involved in being an AAU official at track and field meets on the high school and college-level—Jadwin Stadium in Princeton, Brendon Byrne Arena in New Jersey's Meadowlands, Madison Square Garden, among others.

Marty Glickman was a neighbor of Woodruff when he was living in New Rochelle. The sports broadcast legend, Syracuse football star, and former runner who was a member of the 1936 Olympic team but never got a chance to compete, having been dropped because he was a Jew, knew Woodruff as a dignified, solemn-looking man. "His son and my son played on the same little league football team in New Rochelle," Glickman, who died in 2001, once said in his humorous style. "I was yelling like crazy, and John was standing there quietly."

John had often said, "I love to be involved with kids in athletics, to be a role model and friend to them. That's why I like officiating."

For generations of runners, John has served as a role model—and for many, as a friend. Until their deaths, John maintained relationships with fellow athletes Jesse Owens and Ralph Metcalfe. John inspired many unknown to him. For years he was a popular speaker at the Peddie School near his New Jersey home advising students to "get an education, have the courage, and never give up."

University of Mississippi historian Charles Ross summed it up nicely, "All the athletes represented a generation of pioneers who chiseled away at stereotypes. You have to have Jesse Owens, John Woodruff, and the other sixteen African-Americans before you can have John Carlos, Ali, or George Foreman."

Old John was once asked to sum up his selfless manner:

"I always tried to apply my energies for the good of society, and to maintain my humbleness, regardless of my achievements. What do some call it? Walk softly but carry a big stick? And no matter how difficult a situation I find myself in, I try to be a missionary of sorts, helping people along the way, making sure I leave my mark that way. And by helping people also in difficult social circumstances. I really have enjoyed taking an interest in others and caring for their progress in life, no matter where they come from. Like the *Sporting Image* article said of me, I guess it's in my DNA, and I'm glad for that. Helping others gives me a great feeling."

CHAPTER 58

New York, 1960

John always kept his keen interest in rehabilitation work among young people, especially those who have run afoul of the law. People felt something extraordinary about John that went beyond running. They, too, were attracted to his "honest self," the greatest gift one person can give to another. The core of John—that quiet, forceful, and susceptible sweet spot—made people put their trust in him.

John, as a social investigator and parole officer in New York's Harlem district, went searching for a felon who had jumped bail. Upon locating the violator upstate, John's job was to bring him back to the "Sing-Sing" prison in Ossining, New York. Woodruff's soft, soothing words have the runaway felon guy surrendering without an incident. The captor was put in the caged security of a police car's back seat and driven back to justice.

Inside the parole vehicle, John looked through the rearview mirror at his caged lawbreaker. "Don't think your life is at a dead-end, Diego. You can still make it."

The captive, unruly youth, was depressed. "How? I can't get a job, got no education, no money, no nothin' but a rap sheet."

"But, you do have something: me!"

Diego looked surprised.

"When we get back," John continued, "I'll visit you in jail, help get you squared away."

"Yeah, right. You gotta name?"

"John Woodruff. I'll work with you. And not just a one-shot deal. Three times a week, 'til you make it or break it."

Diego weighed what the officer was saying. "What's the catch? Like all you gotta do is bring me in and your job's done."

"Let's say that I like to keep on the good side of the Big Man." John pointed upward to the heavens.

"So, you ended up a parole officer runnin' after convicts like me. It seems to me, God short-changed you!"

Woodruff decided to use a different tact. "You have some muscle. You lift the iron?"

Diego relaxed some, glad for the compliment.

"Yeah, I love to pump the iron when not on the run."

Woodruff calculated. "Here's my deal: you work with me on finding a skill to your liking. Maybe a job cleaning up the prison weight room. Once you do your required work, you can spend your free time lifting."

Diego considered Woodruff's words. "Everyone talks it up how they're gonna help, but then forget all about it. Why should you be any different?"

"I see your future being clean and successful," Woodruff surprised him. "If I'm wrong, then I wasted my time. And I should know, you see, I once had a record as well."

"What they get you for?"

"Speeding," Woodruff said. "I set some world record."

Diego smirked. "Man, where'd they find you? I mean, don't ya got somethin' better to do?"

"I'm all you've got. If you want my time, it's yours."

There was another silence in the car. Finally: "How fast were you goin', man?" Diego asked.

John emitted a chuckle. "Pretty fast."

A couple of days later, Woodruff visited Diego in jail, the strapping youth surprised but glad to see him. After John observed Diego cleaning out the weight room and sneaking in some heavy reps with weights, he took the kid to the library—a foreign place to the criminal. There, John began helping Diego improve his reading abilities. Before Woodruff left the prison, they went back to the weight room where he spotted Diego as he performed a heavy bench press.

"Way to go, Big D," encouraged John.

One year later, Parole Officer Woodruff was coming out of a Harlem restaurant. Diego was across the street. The huge "Big D" literally ran across the street to confront John, stopping traffic as he did. Pedestrians sensed a physical confrontation about to take place. However, Long John just stood there with a satisfied look, waiting to be accosted.

Big Diego bear-hugged his unlikely friend.

Big D shouted, "Long John. My man! I got myself a weight trainer job at a big health club. Good pay, an' I love it."

"I expected as much, D."

"You're the only one who ever believed in me. I owe ya."

Woodruff considered this. "Yes you do. But I just had a pancake stack an' eggs, so you got away free of charge."

"Come on, Mister Olympic Gold Medal man. How can I pay you back?"

"You're going to run into people throughout life who need help," Woodruff began. "Don't turn your back on them, D. Give them some time; that's all most people need."

Diego clutched Woodruff's hand to seal the deal.

CHAPTER 59

Connellsville, Penna. – under the Woodruff Tree, 2001

Mr. Woodruff was asked if he ever returned to Berlin after the Olympics.

In 1986, John recalled being invited to Berlin to celebrate the 50th anniversary of its Games. "I guess if Jesse Owens were living, he would've gone, but because he was dead, they invited my wife and me. And they showed us a very nice time for the four days we were there."

John remembered quite well that time in a Berlin dignitary hall when he was seventy-one years old and with his attractive and equally-as-kind wife, Rose. At one of the ceremonies for the ex-Olympic medal-winning athletes, they walked into a room full of dignitaries.

"*Achtung. . . Achtung*," A German official announced. "Attention . . . Attention! Ladies and gentlemen, I present the 1936 Gold Medal 800-meter winner, John Woodruff!"

The Woodruff's visited the Berlin Wall, Tiergarten Park, Brandenburg Gate, and also the old Olympic Village on the edge of Berlin, which was now abandoned and in a tattered state of disrepair continuing to rot away, left to return to the mists of its ambiguous past.

It was when John passed by the area of chancellery ground where, fifty-five feet under it in a bunker, Adolph Hitler and Joseph Goebbels committed suicide forty-one years ago.

John remembered saying to his wife, "Hitler claimed his empire would last for a thousand years, and it lasted only for twelve. Let's just hope that evil like him is never seen by the world again."

John Woodruff with one of his many First Place running trophies. (Courtesy of
University of Pittsburgh.)

Woodruff also went inside the place that held the most importance—
the Berlin Stadium, where John had run gloriously in 1936. He knew
well that the Olympic Stadium was used as an underground bunker in
World War II as the war went against Nazi Germany's favor.

"I'm looking out at that empty Olympic stadium," old John recalled,
"and I had a quick flash. Suddenly, I could see all those flags and the
soldiers marching, and I could imagine all those people. High up on

1936 empty Berlin Stadium postcard.

my right was the Chancellor's box, where Hitler and the Nazi leadership watched me. For a second, there were over a hundred thousand people in the place again, the air filled with the smell of beer and frankfurters, and I was running. It was like yesterday. Nearly seventy years ago, Hitler would not greet me or shake my hand. But on that 1986 trip, every dignitary in Germany wanted to shake my hand."

John recalled being with a group of former track-and-field stars in a celebration marking the 65th anniversary of the 1936 Olympic Games in Berlin. The poster in the background—an Aryan athlete as he rides atop a carriage with an Aryan staff in his hands led by four horses—was reflective of Hitler's obsession to create a Nordic "master race."

Old John recalled, "Rose and I toured Berlin visiting places I'd been with my Olympic teammates. Nothing looked the same; it was a new and different country, but the memories were still alive inside me."

It was shocking for Woodruff to see the Olympic Village, on the edge of Berlin where he stayed with all the other athletes during the eight days of the 1936 Games. The once majestic complex had remained in ruins since the war. For fifty years, Soviet forces occupied the ground. The barracks remain, but rotting away.

When Woodruff viewed the huge by empty and decrepit dining hall, he had a flash of eating there during the Olympics, the Olympic Village architect, Captain Wolfgang Fuerstner, passing by on several occasions to make sure Long John was getting his fill of spaghetti.

It became sad for the elder Woodruff knowing that the man found to come from a Jewish background forced to resign from the military committed suicide right after the Olympics.

CHAPTER 60

Atlanta Olympic Games, 1996

Olympic champ John Woodruff was also a guest of honor at the Atlanta Olympic Games in '96. He was able to see Gretel Bergmann-Lambert, Marty Glickman, and some other old former athlete friends. Some former Olympians made up the panel in front of a packed crowd. Sitting on each side of him was Marty Glickman and Gretel, who was then eighty-two.

John Woodruff with dear athletic friends Marty Glickman and Gretel Bergmann-Lambert at a 1996 Atlanta Olympics guest speaking panel.

"I wasn't going to accept this invitation," Gretel shared with her two good American friends, "but my family urged me. They said it was time to move on. I guess they're right. Maybe make the ghosts of the past a little less unfriendly."

"They're right," John agreed. "I've also moved on."

Gretel added, "The young people of Germany shouldn't be held responsible for what their elders did."

Glickman was uncharacteristically serious when saying, "When I returned to Berlin and walked into the stadium, I began to get so angry. I began to get so mad. It shocked the heck out of me that this thing of forty-nine years ago could still evoke my anger. I was cussing and amazed at myself at this feeling of anger. Not about the German Nazis, that was a given, but the anger was at Avery Brundage and Dean Cromwell for not allowing an eighteen-year-old kid to compete in the Olympic Games just because he was Jewish."

Glickman then flipped on his humor switch. "And when I was in the Berlin Stadium, I looked up at the box where Hitler once sat and yelled, 'I'm here, and you're not!'"

His quip had him sharing a laugh with Woodruff and Gretel.

Gretel then serious when addressing Woodruff. "John, we have something in common. I heard the stories of going off to college with all your money—twenty-five cents."

"Yeah," the venerated John answered with a chuckle. "It weighed down my pockets!"

"When I emigrated to America right after the Olympics," Gretel went on, "on the boat ride over, I had all my money with me in my pocket—four dollars. Upon arriving, I went to work as a masseuse and housemaid. Sometimes being that poor makes one strive to be the best."

"I do believe it helped to make us better," John agreed.

"But you, with only twenty-five cents in your pocket going to the University of Pittsburgh," Glickman said with a grin. "I mean, don't spend it all in one place!"

CHAPTER 61

Connellsville, Penna. – under the Woodruff Tree, 2001

John told his young listener how important it felt for him to have come back one more time to the July race in his honor. "God willing, I hope to make it back again next year. This place is my home."

He displayed an extra sense of personal pride when telling that in the 11th John Woodruff 5K race, two of his granddaughters—Delaia Woodruff, who was thirteen at the time and Leslie Gilliam, fifteen, ran in it. And earlier race coordinators like John Ruggeri and some others would be as proud as John over how this race continued to gain in popularity.

John took a deep breath before adding: "My life often has been portrayed as a man of legendary proportions," he said softly. "But I'm only human and a very old one. If God says that it's my time, then I'm ready. I've always tried the best I could at something, and always presented myself as a gentleman."

"You have, "the teen girl said. "You always ran toward your dream while outrunning a lot of disappointments that would've dragged down a lesser man. And you never made a penny with your athletic talents. Your ledger sheet seems terribly unbalanced."

John thought about that. "My wife Rose says the same, that with all that I've been through, I bear it extremely well. One thing I know for sure, I was born with a natural ability to run."

The talk shifted to The John Woodruff 5K Run and Walk. John said "The earlier race coordinators like John Ruggeri and some others from Connellsville that often helped me in arriving here, such as Doctor Richard Grimaldi, would be as proud as I am at how this race continues to gain in popularity."

John informed her that Dr. Grimaldi had helped to fly John and his wife back to Connellsville and that they often stayed at the doctor's home when in town.

John's silver and gold medals should also be awarded to the twelve-person *John Woodruff Committee,* whose diligent work of preparation began early each year, culminating in presenting each participant a long-sleeve shirt and an imprinted glass each containing the silhouette of John's victory finish.

John told the youth how he had retired with his wife to just outside of Phoenix at Fountain Hills, Arizona, to live in an assisted living facility where they had a spacious apartment. John had two children from his earlier marriage, five grandchildren, and three great-grandchildren.

Woodruff then became quiet, reflecting, as he looked about the Connellsville stadium. On this hot July day, the big tree from Germany provided some relief with a breeze. The conversation between the old Olympic great and the young teen girl switched to today's modern athletes and how they differ from those in Woodruff's days.

"The fame and glory for winning a Gold Medal are still there for today's athletes," Woodruff assessed., "But the difference now is money."

He was voicing his opinion on what has become a sore spot with him—the use of professional athletes in the Games. While other countries have subsidized their athletes, the US entries were amateurs until the 1992 Games when professionals represented this country in Olympic basketball.

"Unlike today's amateur Olympic athletes who many times are amateur only in name," John continued, "there was no allowance given by USOC officials when I ran in '36. Winners received medals, and that was it. Today, they receive much more. I was born too soon. I could have possibly qualified for a great deal of money if I had been born later, and still won the gold medal."

The young teen athlete agreed that if any of them would someday make the Olympics, they would be competing against professionals. They also talked about how, in today's track, the gold medal was everything. A silver medal for second place and a bronze for third did not get endorsement contracts. It was all about marketability. The once noble Olympic idea, 'the ultimate is not to win, but to take part," is all but gone. Unfortunately, the signature of track and field had become individuality—my race, my time, my money.

John further lamented. "All professional people come out now because the only policy they have now is to win, regardless of how."

It all started in the 1988 Games when America's basketball team, coached by John Thompson, lost out. "The country was so determined to win the gold medal in the next Games," John recalled, "that they brought in all those multimillionaire pro players and the other countries didn't have a chance.

"So, they're incorporating professional boxers, professional tennis players, professional basketball players," Woodruff added. "Now the year that Michael Jordan and Charles Barkley professionally played; they were all multi-millionaires. They only had one amateur on that team, a college boy, but he didn't even get a chance to play because the Olympics before that they lost, and they made sure they weren't going to lose again. Basketball opened up the floodgates. So that's a trend now, you see."

The girl asked, "So in your opinion, pro athletes ruin what is the true spirit of the Olympics?"

The old Olympian nodded. "Most definitely. I hardly ever watch the Olympics anymore because of that. I'm happy for them, but me? I didn't earn a penny. But I haven't been forgotten."

John went on, "When I went to the Munich Olympics as a guest, I heard that there might be a boycott by the black athletes I almost decided to forget about the entire trip. There was a possibility that fourteen nations were going to pull out of the Games. If they did, I wasn't going to make the trip. I didn't want just to see part of the Olympics. I wanted to see the best."

The mood continued to be serious when the track legend talked about a dark aspect that crept into the Olympics starting in 1972 and also threatened the 2004 Athens Olympics—terrorism. The Munich Games were infamously known for the massacre of Israeli athletes by Palestinian terrorists.

"The German government couldn't have prevented the killing of the Jewish athletes," John decided. "There was total confusion there because nobody ever expected anything like that to happen. The Germans were dealing with a bunch of fanatics. The only way that an episode like that can be stopped is more precautionary methods taken in future Games."

Since the massacre had occurred early in the morning, everything had happened before John arrived at the stadium. "The terrorists made a big publicity thing out of it, wanting the world to focus on what they were doing."

In past years, some countries had boycotted the Games, particularly the United States in 1980, Russia in 1984, and many African nations had threatened to do it before South Africa was allowed to compete.

"There's no place for politics in the Olympic Games," old John said adamantly. "But unfortunately, it has crept in to turn what was once a worldwide competition into one of nationalism.

"Every country should participate," he figured. "It was unfortunate that we didn't enter in 1980, at Moscow, because the Russians had invaded Afghanistan. This created a handicap and a big disappointment, for the young athletes who trained so hard for these Games and then could not compete.

"But that was what President Carter wanted to do," he continued. "He felt it would get back at the Russians, but the Russians just retaliated with their boycott and didn't come to Los Angeles in 1984. I know that all Olympians want to compete against the best, and the best wasn't there in 1984 because East Germany and Russia weren't there, and they have some of the best athletes in the world."

Nationalism had crept into the Games just as other political struggles, such as left against right and communism against capitalism had as well. But it was not always that way. It had become America against the other athletes from other countries to see who was best. It seemed as if this nationalism started in 1952 when Russia entered for the first time, and it had persisted.

The Athens Games were talked about next. A wrestler from Iran withdrew instead of competing against an Israeli wrestler because he refused to accept Israel as a country. Israeli athletes had an additional layer of security at the Olympic Village, including a fence placed around the team's residential compound.

"The Olympics are supposed to be something great," Woodruff believed. "I know how fortunate I felt to be a part of them in '36. I hope the athletes can feel the same way in the future."

Another subject came up in which John was sensitive: past athletic performance versus the present day.

"All my records have been broken by much better times," he continued. "However, the old records were set on cinders, and now they run on artificial surfaces. The pole vaulters of my time, and long afterward, used bamboo poles, but today they have fiberglass poles that catapult today's vaulter over the bar. However, I hold no grudges. I was a product of my time.

"Everything's so much better for the athletes today," Woodruff went on. "They train better, eat better, and their facilities and equipment are so much better. The track shoe athletes wear today don't weigh as much as one of my shoes, with a steel layer in the sole, weighed. There's a more scientific approach to training. That's progress. There are many more incentives for youngsters to be good athletes today."

The conversation under the Woodruff Tree veered to one the old Olympian detested: illegal performance-enhancing drugs.

"It's terrible what you kids are subjected to today," he lamented. "It's destroying our youth. I read a comprehensive survey in *US News and World Report* stating that nearly twenty percent of college kids in America are involved in drugs, and it's getting in high schools and grade schools, too. We know what drugs have done to pro sports. And track and field? Our sport's credibility is dangerously at risk."

"So you wouldn't have taken steroids or other performance-enhancing drugs if they had been available in your day?"

"Most definitely not," he answered with conviction.

"What if all your competition in 1936 Berlin was taking illegal drugs to run faster against you? Would that had made you take them?"

"No. I always strived to have a good reputation no matter what I got involved in," John explained. "One's reputation is perhaps the most prized attribute a person possesses. To lose that is to lose your innocence. I'd be so humiliated if I won a race only for people to wonder if I won it with the help of some illegal drug. No, I'd never risk taking them for that reason, not to mention drugs that can harm an athlete's health."

The talk under the Woodruff Tree turned to repeat some experts' opinion that track and field were dead nowadays. The constant buzz in the sports world was that drug scandals had made everyone suspect. Athletes cannot wait for the day when people come up to them after a race and ask them about their performance, not what they think about drugs. The public realized that the world of track and field had become a dirty business and that it goes far beyond just the coaches and athletes. It also involves businessmen and chemists using "undetectable" designer steroids, human growth hormones, and blood doping to defraud their fellow competitors and the American and world public who pay to attend sporting events. Athletes at the 1996 Atlanta Olympics joked that the event should have been renamed the "Growth Hormone Olympics."

Athletes today are larger, stronger, and faster than those of Woodruff's days. The weight men weigh 50-100 pounds more with the greater muscle mass that makes them more durable. The runners are also much faster.

"In my day, we had it rough in other ways," John assessed. "But you athletes have to decide within yourself: to cheat or not to cheat. Cheating may help you get a short-term victory, but eventually, it will turn into a long-term defeat for your character."

They continued to discuss drugs and supplements used to build mass and strength, such as anabolic steroids. Other illegal aids for runners included blood doping techniques and artificial oxygen carriers—the practice of infusing whole blood into an athlete to have better oxygen delivery to the tissues.

It seemed when the testers finally detect a new drug and reprimand an athlete, the laboratories had invented another non-detectable drug in this game of cat and mouse. And the mouse is winning.

The teen asked, "I don't take drugs, but how can I compete later on if I don't use them?"

Old John understood the problem. It was now possible that two athletes with identical skills can be separated by the technology that was available to them.

"I'm an old man with old fashioned beliefs," he said slowly. "Honesty's the best policy, always was, always will be. And the US anti-doping agency is working hard to root out cheaters and those individuals who encourage them. As long as they continue to ban drug-abusing athletes from track and field and other sports, the athletes realize there is too much to lose if they cheat and get caught. It can ruin one's career for life. Just look at the athletes being caught and not allowed to race—some for two years, others have a lifetime ban. No, don't take drugs. The stakes are too high; it's playing Russian roulette."

John added with emphasis, "No one, absolutely no one, should deny any honest, talented runner his or her rightful place on the starting line."

CHAPTER 62

Connellsville, Penna. – under the Woodruff Tree, 2001

The young girl asked John if he held a grudge with his alma mater, the University of Pittsburgh.

The venerated Olympian took his time formulating an answer. "It took Pitt until 1966—thirty years after the Berlin Olympics—before the university gave me the Varsity Letterman of Distinction Award. I was hurt before that. Here I was, the only Olympic champion in the history of the school at the time, yet I was not in Pitt's Hall of Fame in the school yearbook. People like footballer Marshall Goldberg, Curly Stebbins, and John Chickerneo—all classmates of mine—were in, but I wasn't. Those guys brought national recognition to Pitt. I brought the school *international* recognition."

John did admit that Pitt had done its best to make up for the slight, and Woodruff, in turn, remained fiercely loyal to the university.

The teen listener spoke up, "Some say you were in a league of your own. Many people have a lot of respect for those other great Pennsylvania athletes, but none of them braved Hitler's Reich as you did!"

It became known that John Woodruff was the first inductee in the Fayette County Freedom Hall of Fame, before such heroes as World War II General George C. Marshall.

John merely shrugged in recognition of that accolade. He talked more of Pitt, admitting that the university would always have a large piece of his heart.

John Woodruff at University of Pittsburgh football game with his Olympic
Gold Medal. (Courtesy of University of Pittsburgh.)

"I don't hold any grudges," he insisted. "My wounds have healed. It's
been a long time since all that Pitt and other racial stuff happened. It's in
the past, and it doesn't bother me when reminded of it. I even began to
help and encourage some young promising athletes to enter Pitt."

"Because Pitt never had anyone do for them what you did," the teen
voiced. "And there are many people besides me who feel you distinguished yourself and made Pitt proud."

John talked about an article that was in a University of Pittsburgh
Q&A series talking about one black athlete in particular—Roger Kingdom. The slender but muscular Georgia native entered the University
of Pittsburgh in the early '80s on a football scholarship. Roger told of

watching old film footage of John Woodruff's incredible victory run in the '36 Olympics. It deeply moved the young athlete.

Years later, Kingdom did an interview. Beside him was John Woodruff, in his eighties and with a cane.

"When I got to Pitt," Kingdom said to the sportswriter conducting the interview, "I was so much like a butterfly flitting from one thing to the next. I had so much talent and was here on a football scholarship. But to see the videotape of John Woodruff's competition back in the 1936 Olympics made me want to win a medal."

And win medals he did. Kingdom won the Olympic Gold medal in 1984 and '88 in the 100-meter high hurdles.

Roger motioned to Woodruff. "When you sit down and listen to this man, and you hear his stories about all the different directions his life could have gone in, you sit there in awe. That's what John Woodruff does to me. He makes me trip, man. Just following your path has been an inspiration for me. Talking to John Woodruff, I was like a kid in a candy shop."

John shook his head. "I'm glad I've contributed in some way, Roger," Woodruff responded. "And now you have replaced me as Pitt's greatest Olympian ever."

"I don't know about that," Roger says. "You've made the Pitt Hall of Fame, the Pennsylvania Hall of Fame, the Negro Hall, the Track and Field Hall of Fame . . . all of them."

On the ground floor of Pitt's Hillman Library, John Woodruff's 1936 Olympic Gold Medal is hanging on a wall next to the elevators, about a dozen paces down from the restrooms. The award was encased in glass on a plain, wooden plaque about the size of a laptop computer. Its placement is not easy to spot, even for those who go there specifically to see it.

Roger Kingdom said about that medal placed there: "I hope they will create a better display for something so magnificent so everyone can understand the true meaning of this Gold Medal. It's about someone who dedicated his life to be the best, someone who had to fight discrimination and endure great trials to survive and prevail."

Old John was touched by Kingdom's words. At that time, John was sixty-three in New York City at the Waldorf Astoria Hotel, becoming elected into the National Track and Field Hall of Fame.

Dignitaries presented a plaque to the winner of the "John Woodruff 880-yard run," an idea fostered by his friend, another former Pitt Olympic medal winner, Herbert Douglas, a Pitt Emeritus Trustee. In 1945, Herb Douglas became the first African American (along with Jimmy Joe Robinson and Allan Carter) to play football at Pitt.

Douglas addressed the crowd, "John deserves something like this."

Douglas, also a former AAU champion, knew Jesse Owens. He continued, "When I was young, John Woodruff and Jesse Owens influenced me during the 1930s. Most colleges back then didn't allow blacks to play basketball or football, and I was good at those sports. But I knew if I could excel in track and field, I could get an education. Like John Woodruff here with me now—that was something I wanted badly."

Douglas added, "To me, John never reached his peak in running because World War II, and his service in it, intervened. Had there not been a war, he would most likely have won the 800 meters in both the 1940 and 1944 Olympic Games. John's ability was unmatched in the 800 meters, and if the US team had used John in 1936 in the four-by-four relay, the United States would have won the Olympic gold medal in that event as well. As it was, his race was the most spectacular one in the 1936 games.

"John had to overcome many barriers," Douglas continued. "He was very blunt, and an excellent soldier from what I have been able to learn because he'd always go by the book. He was sincere, the epitome of an upright citizen, a moral force, and a compass for me. If something weren't right, he'd sure tell me about it!"

Douglas also had said, "I was a fourteen-year-old emerging football and track star in Pittsburgh when Hitler's Olympics unfolded, a kid who read about the feats of the great Jesse Owens, Archie Williams, and Pitt's John Woodruff in the *Pittsburgh Courier*, perhaps the most influential African-American newspaper in the country. In all, nine African American track athletes hauled in thirteen medals—four of them by Owens.

"It motivated me," Douglas, who now lived in Philadelphia, went on. "It made us believe that we African-Americans—Negroes at the time—could do as well as anybody. We needed that. There were no African Americans in baseball, football, or basketball. We didn't have any idols. Then those Berlin Games came, and it changed everything."

John remembered when it came time for him to speak, he pointed to the large gold ring he was wearing. It acknowledged he was finally gaining admittance to this hallowed group—the Track and Field Hall of Fame.

John brought up to his teen listener that another very memorable moment for him was in May of 1982 at the Pitt Invitational Track and Field Meet, which attracted twenty-five college teams to Pitt Stadium. The university was paying tribute to Hall of Famer John, who wore his prized gold ring. The thundering roar he received from the crowd seemed second only to the applause he had received at the Berlin Stadium Olympics.

"John Woodruff's story was indeed a remarkable one," said Pittsburgh Chancellor Mark A. Nordenberg. "Following the completion of his freshman year at Pitt, he scored a stirring sports and social triumph in the 1936 Berlin Olympics by winning the gold medal in the 800-meter race in what has been called the 'Hitler Olympics.' Because of the social context of his win, as vital as it is in sports history, it was a triumph with far larger implications and even more lasting impact.

"The people in our University community loved and respected John Woodruff," Nordenberg added. "We stood in awe of his athletic achievements, but we also admired him as a human being who helped advance humanity's cause through the values he held and promoted. His lifetime and lifeline of achievements placed him and Pitt in the embrace of the vast and eternal."

Pitt track and field coach Alonzo Webb said, "What an amazing human being he was, and what a legacy he has left for us to marvel at. The shadow he cast was so large and so important that everyone who follows in his footsteps will forever be measured by him and his place in history."

Alonzo Webb added, "A nine-foot stride! That's amazing. I've seen the film of John Woodruff's gold-medal race and marveled at how long his stride was and how smooth he was. A normal stride for an 800-meters runner is about six-and-a-half feet, seven feet at the most."

The teen spoke up again. "I read what your son John Jr. said about you. He said, 'My dad sets little markers. When a grandchild is born, he wants to be there when he graduates high school. He's an indomitable spirit. What he was as an athlete is what he is as a man—just a powerful kind of person with a will and a spirit. My father, for me, was a towering giant. When I think what racism, boundaries, and, later, ill health he went through, it's phenomenal. I now view him very much so, as being my hero.'"

A moist-eyed John looked at this teen alongside him.

"And didn't your son say he could never keep up walking with you, no one could?"

John Woodruff being honored at University of Pittsburgh, October 2006, his last time at his Alma mater. (Courtesy of University of Pittsburgh.)

Old John nodded with a chuckle. "Well, there you have it—the quick version of my story. The many medals and letterman sweater I wore are in Connellsville High School, my gold medal in Pitt's Hillman Library."

From the Woodruff Tree that was a testament to John's courage, an acorn fell from it onto Old John's lap. He held it up, smiling. "I guess this little one needs planting somewhere. I'm going now over to my old friend Pete Salatino's home. Years ago, we planted a seedling from this tree, and it took root. Maybe this acorn will sprout as well."

Rose Woodruff returned for him, touching her husband's shoulder.

"Sorry to interrupt your good time," Rose said. "But we don't want to be late to meet everyone at your old high school."

"Oh, yeah," John said. "I was having such a good time with my little friend here that I forgot about that. Uh, excuse me, I never did get your name?"

"Sarah," the girl said. "Just like your mama's name."

"I love it!" John beamed. "Come join us?"

Sarah grinned in delight.

CHAPTER 63

John Returns to Connellsville High School, 2001

Long John Woodruff wanted to make one more visit to his high school before he would get ready for the start of the John Woodruff 5K race. He was wheeled in with the assistance of his wife and also Sarah inside the entrance hallway of Connellsville High School in front of the handsome glass athletic trophy case on display for students and visitors alike.

As several local photographers snapped off shots of their local hero, the old Olympian reminisced over the various trophies of all the school's sports stars and his many medals, trophies, and photos. In 1976, he turned over his Olympic Gold Medal and some souvenirs of his glorious track career:

- pictures of him with Jesse Owens and Ralph Metcalfe at the 1936 Olympics
- a large photograph of the Olympic Village room where Woodruff stayed while in Berlin
- a photo of Woodruff in his track uniform, others of him winning the Olympic Gold medal
- his Olympic sweater framed and also a part of his track uniform
- four All-American certificates of selection
- citation award accompanying University of Pittsburgh Letterman of Distinction Plaque
- silver 20-inch trophy, gold 17-inch trophy
- Pennsylvania Hall of Fame plaque

- three plaques of Woodruff's first major high school races
- four different framed pictures of Woodruff with his teammates; Pitt track coach, Carl Olsen; and with Connellsville coach, Pops Larew
- 54 medals, framed and mounted on blue velvet

Old John also remembered back in 1976, when he was visiting Connellsville, a group was at the school's cafeteria honoring Woodruff. John was at the podium, presenting his lifetime track honors to the school and its townspeople.

In introducing champion Woodruff, toastmaster James M. Driscoll, president-editor of the town's *Daily Courier*, recalled the first time he saw Woodruff running at old ash-covered, weedy Fayette Field.

Arriving at the microphone to a standing ovation from the 600-plus attendance, sixty-one-year-old Woodruff said, "It is indeed a pleasure for me to be back in Connellsville. I had the pleasure of meeting many of my old friends at our 40th class reunion this year, and I look forward to seeing all of them again in 1980."

John turned his attention to the presentation of his medal, saying: "This is something I have wanted to do for a long time. I had planned to leave them to the school in my Will, but since I plan to be around for a long time, and to inspire youngsters in their athletic endeavors, I've decided to make the presentation now.

"When I was coming along as a young athlete, there wasn't much for us in the way of encouragement. Long-time track official Fred Snell gave me a lot of good advice and encouragement, and Bill Dolde—retired high school coach and principal—is the only one of my old teachers still here . . ."

John returned his thoughts to the present day and said, "I sometimes wonder what direction I might've gone if my Mama hadn't told me to give up football because of the chores I had to do at home." Then he added with a big smile, "And I still wonder just how far I actually ran that Berlin Olympic finals day to win the 800-meter race."

"Was it hard for you to give all your track awards to the school?" Sarah asked.

"No. They've been here for a long time," he said. "After talking with my sister, I was pleased to be able to give all this to the school."

"My Mom died long ago, in 1934," John added fondly. "She didn't live to see what I did in the Olympics or at the University of Pittsburgh. My father did, but then he died in 1940. So, I decided back then to give this track stuff to the school, including that medal. That's the replica of the gold I won in Berlin. You see, I used to have the real one here, but then there was a robbery."

John heard how some devilish kids had broken into the school, and they started destroying the trophy case, the case that held many of the events he had won over the years.

"But they didn't touch my display at all," John assured. "However, the insurance man told the principal to have my Olympic Gold Medal taken out. They gave the medal back to me."

He paused to collect his thoughts. "Until my demise, I felt it might be misplaced," he said. "I wanted it enshrined where it will be secure for all times."

He had presented the Gold Medal to Pitt at the football halftime ceremony in a game against Notre Dame in 1990.

"I took the medal to a jeweler in Princeton," he continued. "He made duplicates from the original medal. And of course, I gave all my granddaughters a duplicate medal with a chain. And I turned over the original medal to the Pitt chancellor."

Sarah also noticed some great professional athletes that went to Connellsville High School, among them the Heisman Trophy winner in college football, Johnny Lujack, who went on to play for the Chicago Bears in the NFL and the league's Hall of Fame.

"Mr. Woodruff," she said to Old John. "Did you know that your name and Johnny Lujack are in the game *Trivial Pursuit?*"

Old John looked confused. "Uh, no, I didn't. What—?

"A question card for the game asks: 'What city has had both an Olympic Gold Medal winner and also a Heisman Trophy Winner?'"

"Connellsville!" Old John beamed. "You can clearly see what some used to call a hick town is hardly that. There just might be something special in the waters of our Youghiogheny River!"

Long John, Old John, Olympic Gold Medal, and the iconic Woodruff Tree, Connellsville, PA archives.

CHAPTER 64

Connellsville, 2001

As the Woodruff's and Sarah were driven back to the stadium to drop her off, she asked John, "Can you stay one minute, maybe a few seconds longer to watch something?"

John and Rose looked to one another in puzzlement.

"Sure, Sarah, but to watch what?"

"Thanks. Want to show you something."

She rushed out of the car door to spring onto the track. Sarah took off running a lap, *really* running her 440-yard lap with a long precision stride.

"Lordy, Lordy," Old John exclaimed. "That young one sure can stretch her limbs, runs like the wind!"

Sarah finished her lap in just over a minute. She came over to the car and Old John.

"Are you aware of how good you are, Sarah?"

She nodded with confidence. "I know I'm good, but I want to be even better."

"Sarah, don't waste your talent, find your way," John insisted. "Live your dream."

John Woodruff received a hug from Sarah, a final goodbye.

However, the youth did not seem to want to let go of Woodruff, asking, "You said you were a gifted athlete. Did you need much coaching?"

"That's partially true," John responded. "You can't teach a natural runner much about running. But the coaches I had wanted me to do well, and they encouraged me. Coaches kept me on a schedule."

It was evident that the teen did not want to leave. "Did you ever coach runners?"

"No, not particularly," John answered. "When I was going to NYU graduate school, I was helping Coach Videl with his boys, but that's about as far as I ever went with it. I never thought of coaching as a job."

"Are there any runners today or in the last twenty years that remind you of your style, and your speed?"

"No, you don't see any tall, long-legged runners out there now. Some medium-high fellows. You know, I was kind of an exception, 'cause I was tall for a runner."

It was evident to John that the girl was still searching for more of his advice. "You have to work hard to get what you want," the Olympian added, "To achieve great things, you have to believe in two people above all others—God and yourself. Be prepared for sacrifice. Nothing's going to come too easy. Take instruction. You have to travel a long and hard road. In many ways, you grow stronger when what you try to accomplish doesn't come too easy. If you appreciate your struggles, you then go on to higher achievements."

John smiled. "The thing about the Olympics is, it's just like it happened yesterday. It impresses one, particularly as a young athlete. The things that you see walking in with your team in the parade, and the camaraderie you develop with your team members, you don't forget those things. We created history in Berlin, and you can't argue with the facts."

Old John found that the teen girl had worked to open his heart up, him telling that when sprinter Archie Williams died, his passing left John the last surviving track and field Gold Medalist from that 1936 team. Cornelius Johnson died at the age of 32 shortly after the Olympics. Ralph Metcalfe, who went on to become a congressman, died the year before Jesse Owens had passed on.

"I'm proud to have the status," Woodruff admitted, "but I'm sad to think about the many good men that died to make me the last survivor.

We were all very close, having a special friendship that lasted through the years, long after the Games. We stayed in touch with each other."

"And this happened to you—in the hick town of Connellsville!" the teen quipped.

John broke into a huge grin to answer, "Yes, and dirt poor as well."

"Yet that dirt produced gold, a gold medal!" the teen said with pride. "And you carved yourself a spot in history!"

The smiling old Olympian touched the girl's hand in goodbye before the car he was in drove away.

After attending the John Woodruff 5K race that early evening to fire the signal to start the race, Old John felt so good being back to his roots, seeing old friends and, of course, the young running hopefuls. He already began to look forward to returning next year. But as fate would have it, this would be the last time he would see his beloved Connellsville.

Fountain Valley, Arizona, 2002

Old John's health began to deteriorate. It started when he had fallen and broken his hip. That was followed by him developing pneumonia and a urinary tract infection, both of which agitated his neuropathy, a nerve disorder—in his case, brought on by poor circulation. That poor circulation began eating away at his legs. The condition worsened to the point that the doctors said they might be able to save one of his legs but offered no guarantee. It was decided that amputating both his legs at the knees was the best course of action. The man with the longest-running stride ever recorded, was no more.

"What an irony and tragedy, huh?" asked John Lucas, the Olympic movement's foremost historian. "'The guy with the longest legs and the fastest legs.'"

Long John's last public appearance was on April 15, 2007, when he, along with the members of the Tuskegee Airmen, was honored by the Arizona Diamondbacks by throwing out the first pitch.

John Woodruff holding a photo of him winning the Berlin Gold. (Courtesy of Melissa Cooper, 2006, *New York Times*.)

Woodruff returned to his Arizona home with one regret. His doctor had advised him to give up dreams of seeing one last time the oak tree in Connellsville that commemorated his Olympic glory. Another trip like that was just too much.

"But that's okay," John told his wife and friends. "For a man my age, I'm feeling pretty good. I have no complaints."

At his bedside was a small stack of biography and history books, plus his trusty Bible.

Woodruff died Tuesday at a center in Fountain Hills, said Rose Woodruff, his wife of 37 years. He was 92. "I was at his bedside at the time he passed," she said. "We were holding hands, and he slipped away peacefully."

Mrs. Woodruff added, "He had a wonderful life. John was a good man, a good person, and had much integrity and a very strong character."

John Woodruff is buried at Crown Hill Cemetery, Indianapolis, Indiana (section 46, lot 86).

Epilogue

John Woodruff was honored in Feb. 2007 during a ceremony in Dallas. In 1937, he smashed the world record in the 800-meter at the Pan Am Games only to have officials rule the track six feet short of regulation. That same year, students in Texas set up a mathematical equation showing that Mr. Woodruff, even if the track had been extended to regulation length, would still have beaten Robinson's record by a second-and-a-half. Experts often call it the biggest racing injustice in track history.

The Tribune Live in 2007 covered a Memorial for John Woodruff of almost a hundred people gathered at the "re-named" Connellsville Falcon Stadium—John Woodruff Track/John Lujack Field on a Sunday afternoon to honor the memory of Connellsville's Olympic gold medalist John Woodruff.

Among those attending included two past Olympic gold medalists, a university chancellor, family members, public officials, and friends. The track star, a veteran of two wars, and humanitarian died Oct. 30, 2007. He was ninety-two.

The memorial service at Falcon Stadium was Woodruff's request. It was near the oak tree that grew from a sapling that Woodruff brought home from the 1936 Berlin Olympics.

The South Connellsville native was twenty years old and a University of Pittsburgh student when he made his way across the ocean to compete in the Olympics in Germany.

Woodruff Club member Fayette County Judge John Wagner Jr. introduced the speakers. University of Pittsburgh Chancellor Mark A. Nordenberg was keynote speaker.

"Raised here in Connellsville, John Woodruff left high school as a teen to try and find a job to help out at home, but he quickly returned to school when he could not find one," said Mr. Nordenberg. "He took up running and soon held school, county, district, and state records."

After Woodruff set the country's best time for running a mile, a group of local businessmen helped put together a scholarship to get him into Pitt.

"He arrived on campus with just a quarter in his pocket and began to hit the books and the track," Nordenberg said.

At the Olympics, Woodruff ran the 800 meters in 1:52.9, claiming the gold medal. He was the first of five African Americans, including the legendary Jesse Owens, to win gold medals in Berlin.

"Despite the myth of Arian supremacy in athletics by the Nazis, that collective triumph will always live on as a victory for the forces of good," Nordenberg said.

State Sen. Richard Kasunic called those feats the first victories toward a free world for the countries that would ally themselves against Germany when World War II started a few years later.

"John Woodruff was a true hero, and we should all take a page out of his life," Kasunic said. "If we did, this would certainly be a better, kinder, gentler world that we live in."

Nordenberg added that Woodruff's spirit would never die in Western Pennsylvania. "His memory will live on our campus, and his legacy will certainly live on from the memory of the oak tree that he brought back from Germany's Black Forest and planted here more than seventy years ago," he said.

Local author Ceane O'Hanlon Lincoln, who was asked a year before Woodruff's death to deliver the eulogy at his memorial service, said the oak tree planted in Connellsville is one of the few surviving trees from the saplings presented to participants in the 1936 Olympics.

"John Woodruff was the epitome of the great human spirit that came along in the right moment of time, to inspire hundreds of thousands of people worldwide," she said. "He was a winner and a warrior on the track and in life."

Herb Douglas and Roger Kingdom, both Woodruff protégés who won Olympic gold medals, spoke of their friend.

"Back then, there were no Jackie Robinsons or Michael Jordans," Douglas said. "People like Johnny Woodruff and Jesse Owens were our heroes."

Kingdom, who won the gold medal in the hurdles competition in the 1984 and 1988 Olympics, said Woodruff meant much to him.

"One of the things you never heard from him when he talked about his experiences was negative," he said. "Because of that, I set my goal to make the Olympic team, and I just held on to that. And when a person has a goal and a mission, they're like a rock that's hard to move."

Woodruff's son, John Youie Woodruff Jr., recalled how much his father loved his hometown. "My father obviously loved this city, and I thank you for honoring a man who distinguished himself and whom I've often said was my hero," he said.

John Woodruff's widow, Rose, was presented with proclamations from Kasunic, State Rep; Debra Kula, Fayette County Commissioner; Angela Zimmerlink; and U.S. Rep. William Shuster.

"He was a gentleman, a scholar and an athlete," said Joe Turek, former Connellsville Area High School track coach and one of the founders of the Woodruff 5K Run & Walk. "He had everything that is best in people: generosity, a love for kids, a love for education."

Mrs. Woodruff summed up her late husband, succinctly, "My husband was very strong and had great character and integrity. He was a very determined man. He put his whole heart into everything he did."

Like the man himself, the Woodruff Oak remains a towering presence at Connellsville and a symbol of strength and resilience that represents John Woodruff's legacy.

Over seventy years ago, Olympic gold medalist John Woodruff was denied the opportunity to compete in a track meet alongside his

University of Pittsburgh teammates at the US Naval Academy in Annapolis, Md. Due to Maryland's segregation laws, the academy refused to compete in the 1939 event if Woodruff ran, so he was left behind. Two years after Woodruff's death, the Naval Academy issued a public apology to John Woodruff.

Capt. Tony Barnes delivered the message and addressed his words especially to Mrs. Rose Woodruff with his son John Jr., "We would like you to know that all of us here at the Naval Academy apologize and are sorry for what Mister Woodruff faced in the past. This is not a time to cast blame, although certainly many deserve blame. Now is the time to look at our bright future. Our new president reminds us that this is a time to act and act in a manner that will produce change," Barnes said.

The Navy has agreed to plant an offshoot of the Woodruff Tree next to the academy's track.

Black History Month honors African Americans that stood as examples of human possibility. It reminds everyone that we are capable and deserving of the goals, dreams, and accomplishments that are part of every mortal. John Youie "Long John" Woodruff embodies the spirit and purpose of Black History Month.

And true to their promise, the University of Pittsburgh unveiled a new interactive display of John Woodruff on the first floor of Pitt's Hillman Library, 3960 Forbes Ave., Oakland. The six-feet-high exhibition included an interactive Multi-Time Media touch screen featuring film narratives, a photo gallery, and selections from Woodruff's family scrapbook. Most of the materials had never been on public view before. The 1936 Berlin Olympic Gold Medal, which Woodruff donated to Pitt in 1990, was now showcased on a rotating illuminated pedestal.

A White House Tribute at Last

In 2016, President Obama met with the families of the African American athletes of the 1936 Olympic Games in Berlin, offering praise that Franklin Roosevelt did not.

Eighty years later, the athletes, sixteen men, and two women received their overdue recognition by a US President when their relatives visited the White House for an event honoring the US team at the Rio games.

"It wasn't just Jesse. It was other African American athletes in the middle of Nazi Germany under the gaze of Adolf Hitler than put a lie to notions of racial superiority—whooped 'em—and taught them a thing or two about democracy and taught them a thing or two about the American character," President Obama said Thursday.

The other athletes were Dave Albritton, John Brooks, James Clark, Cornelius Johnson, Willis Johnson, Howell King, James LuValle, Ralph Metcalfe, Art Oliver, Tidye Pickett, Fritz Pollard Jr., Mack Robinson, Louise Stokes, John Terry, Archie Williams, Jack Wilson, and John Woodruff. Eighteen relatives attended the White House event and shook the president's hand, according to the AP.

Woodruff, the last surviving member of the 1936 Olympics, has suffered his share of racism—not so much by foreigners but within the confines of the U.S. His story is a reminder of how far we have come.

Post Epilogue

A ghost-like image of a tall runner in shadow loped around the Falcon Stadium track, head held high. The incredible long elastic pace of the legs could only belong to the legendary man from Connellsville, who had the most extended recorded gait ever—Long John Woodruff. The surreal phantom figure glided effortlessly along the track past the magnificent oak tree whose long branches appeared to reach out to him.

Old John's educated and soothing voice was heard: "Legend has it that at the right time of day, you can see the tree's oneness with a black shadow—lengthening in perfect stride."

Appendix A

John Y. Woodruff
by *Fountain Hills Times*, Arizona
November 7, 2007

John Y. Woodruff Sr., resident of Fountain View Village, peacefully departed this life in the early morning hours of Oct. 30, 2007, with his wife, Rose, at his side. He is in the loving arms of our Lord and Savior.

John, the son of Silas and Sarah Woodruff and the grandson of ex-slaves, was born on July 5, 1915, in Connellsville, Pa.

After graduating from Connellsville High School, he applied for a job at a local glass factory but, because of his race, was turned away.

Ironically, this indignity turned out to be a blessing in disguise. Because John had demonstrated such prodigious talent as a track runner in high school, the University of Pittsburgh offered him a full athletic scholarship.

With only 25 cents in his pocket, the sheriff of his hometown drove John to the University of Pittsburgh to begin his new life. In 1939, John received his bachelor's degree in sociology. He later went on to earn a master's degree in sociology at New York University in 1941.

During his tenure, John brought national and international recognition to his alma mater. As a 21-year-old freshman at the University of Pittsburgh, John earned the right to represent the United States in the 1936 Berlin Olympic Games held in Berlin, Germany.

With his fabled 9-plus foot stride, "Long John" outran his competition and won a gold medal in the 800-meter race.

Upon his return to the States, John continued to distinguish himself as a true champion by winning every race he competed in after the Olympic Games including the NCAA 800-meter race in 1937, '38, '39; the ICAAAA 400- and 800-meter race three years in succession; the 800-meters at the Pan American Games and the National AAU Track Meet.

In recognition of his outstanding athletic accomplishments, John has been named to the USA Track and Field Hall of Fame and was the first person to be inducted into the Fayette County Freedom Hall of Fame.

Notably, John was the last surviving Gold Medalist of the 1936 Olympic Games and, since 1982, has sponsored the John Woodruff 5K run/walk, which has raised thousands of dollars that go to fund scholarships for students in his hometown of Connellsville.

John served his country in World War II and the Korean War, retiring as a lieutenant colonel. He was an ROTC instructor at West Virginia State College and, in his civilian life, worked for the New York City Children's Aid Society and taught school.

Also, he was a special investigator for the New York Department of Welfare, a recreational center director for the New York City Police Athletic League and a parole officer for the City of New York. Woodruff was also a sales representative for Shefflin Distributors and retired as a manager for the Job Corp.

In 1942, John married Hattie Mae Davis; deceased. From this union daughter, Randi Gilliam of Chicago and son John Jr. of New York City were born.

While working in Indianapolis, John met and subsequently married Rose Ella King in 1970. Over the course of 37 years of marriage, John and his devoted wife have lived in Sacramento, Calif. and East Windsor, N.J. After retirement, John and Rose moved to Fountain View Village of Fountain Hills in 2002.

John was a legendary track star, but he was truly more than that. He was a deeply religious man, a man of great strength and determination, a man who tried to make a difference in the lives of others and, to some, he was a hero.

He will be greatly missed by family, friends, and main caregivers for several years.

John leaves his wife of 37 years, Rose; daughter, Randi; son, John; grand-children Hope, Alexis, Leslie, Dalila and Jelani; daughter-in-law Dafua; brother-in-law William; great-grandchildren; and many friends and extended family to cherish his memory.

A memorial service was held Saturday, Nov. 3, 2007, at Fountain View Village Independent Living Chapel.

Appendix B

THE WOODRUFF RECORD
(Athletic highlights)

HIGH SCHOOL
- Pennsylvania high school record, June 1935—4:23.4, Pitt Stadium

COLLEGE – UNIVERSITY OF PITTSBURGH
Freshman
- Second National A.A.U. to Beetham of Ohio State
- Won Olympic Trials in 800—1:49.9
- Won Berlin Olympics 880 Gold Medal (first American since Ted Meredith) 1:52.9
- Anchored Sprint Medley and Two-Mile Relay teams in British Empire Games

Sophomore
- Won National A.A.U. 880 (new record 1:50)
- Won ICAAAA 440 and 880 (tied record of :47 in 440)
- Won NCAA 800 (new record 1:50.3)
- Won Pan American 880 at Dallas (1:47.8 for new unofficial world record)
- Won the Compton, Calif. Invitational 400-meters 47 seconds.
- Anchored Winning Sprint medley team to equal American record (3:26.4 Penn Relays)

Junior
- Won ICAAAA 440 and 880
- Won NCAA 880
- Anchored three winning relay teams at Penn Relays—Sprint Medley 3:24.5 (New American record)
- 880 1:26.6 (Carnival Record)
- Mile 3:17.8

Senior
- Penn Relays—Anchored three championship teams
- Sprint Medley 3:25.8
- 880 1:25.9 (New Carnival Record)
- Mile 3:14.8 (New Carnival Record)
- Indiana Duel Meet—Won Mile at 4:12.

Won following Events:
- 440 :47.0 (Outdoor ICAAAA record)
- 880 1:51.2 (Outdoor ICAAA record)
- 880 1:51.2 (NCAA record)
- 1940 won the Millrose Indoor half-mile race at Madison Square Garden 1:52.8
- World's indoor record 800 meters 1:47.6 Dartmouth College

HONORS
- Member of National Track and Field Hall of Fame, Inducted 1978
- Member of Black Athletes Hall of Fame, Inducted 1978
- Member of Pennsylvania State Hall of Fame, Inducted 1966
- Member of the City of Pittsburgh Hall of Fame, Inducted 1966
- Received the Letterman of Distinction Award from the University of Pittsburgh, 1966
- The first Univ. of Pittsburgh Track All-American, three years in a row
- Univ. of Pittsburgh Athletics Hall of Fame (inaugural 16-member class)

- Intercollegiate American Amateur Athletic Assoc. Champion—three successive years for the quarter and half-mile races 1937-1938–1939 (Breaking 58-year old record) Randall's Island Stadium, New York City
- Fayette Country Freedom Hall of Fame (First inductee)
- Penn Relays Wall of Fame

EDUCATION
- Connellsville High School, graduated 1935
- The University of Pittsburgh, graduated 1939, Major—Sociology
- MA Degree—New York University, graduated 1941, Major–Sociology
- New York University 1947-1948 completed sixteen credit hours in Vocational Guidance and Personnel Administration

EMPLOYMENT
- New York City Children's Aid Society 1940–1941
- New York City Board of Education—(School Teacher) 1945–1946
- New York City Department of Welfare (Social Investigator) 1946–1947
- New York City Police Athletic League (Recreational Center Director) 1947–1948
- New York State Division of Parole (Parole Officer) 1948–1954
- Schieffelin and Company 1954–1955

MILITARY
Army Service
- Entered the service in 1941 as Second Lieutenant. Left in 1945 as Captain.
- Re-entered service (Korean War) Major, 1950. Left service as Lieutenant Colonel in 1957. All of his services was in Artillery.

- Executive Officer of 5 different artillery battalions. Commanded two battalions. (one of the two an integrated battalion).
- All of his services was served in the Far East, beginning from Hawaii, Okinawa, Korea, Japan.

Army Service (Reserves)
- Commanded the 1st Howitzer Battalion (155-mm) SP 369th Combat Arms Regiment, New York Army National Guard. Officer in charge and control of the 369th Infantry Armory located in 2366 Fifth Avenue, Harlem, New York City

OTHER MEMBERSHIPS
- Member: United States Olympians, New York Chapter
- Alpha Phi Alpha Fraternity.
- Deacon John Woodruff, Baptist Church, Edison, New Jersey (near John's former Hightown home)

Additional Acknowledgments

Years ago, while researching Long John the author visited Connellsville and met by chance Mrs. Jessie Salatino. Her deceased husband Pete Salatino was Long John's close childhood friend. Mrs. Salatino invited me into her home. A couple of her friends also joined us, and I heard their many heartwarming stories of John Woodruff that gave me valuable insight into his early Connellsville years.

A special thanks also goes to L. Warner of the *Carnegie Free Library*, Connellsville, who, also years ago, directed the author to countless newspaper and magazine articles about the legendary John Youie Woodruff.

About the Author

David Orange is a veteran Broadway stage and film actor with two co-starring roles on the Broadway stage. He has also appeared in several TV episodic guest star appearances, and in over 300 TV commercials. His feature film roles include the memorable cameo as the *Sleepy Klingon* in the hit film *Star Trek VI- the Undiscovered Country*.

Orange, the writer, has had several novels published including *Mutant Specimen L* by Eternal Press, *Mine Game* by Whiskey Creek Press, and the novella *This Cemetery is Mine* by Web-E-Books and also 25 journalism articles in several wine magazines. Recently, he also has a screenplay optioned, *Portal to Paradise* by Movie Corp.

David was born and raised in the town of Jeannette, Penna. about twenty miles from John Woodruff's Connellsville

Donation

One-third of all net profits paid to the author for sales of the *Long John* biographical novel, both in paperback and EBook, will be donated to the John Woodruff 5K Run and Walk Club to benefit the Annual John Woodruff Scholarship.

CPSIA information can be obtained
at www.ICGtesting.com
Printed in the USA
LVHW092147060221
678613LV00034B/377